THE CASE OF THE STOLEN SCARAB

A CANDLESTONE  INN MYSTERY

by
Nancy Garden

Two Lives Publishing

Published by
Two Lives Publishing
508 N. Swarthmore Avenue
Ridley Park, PA 19078
www.TwoLives.com

ISBN: 0-9674468-7-2

LCCN: 2002109055

1 2 3 4 5 6 7 8 9 10

Printed in Canada

For Maggie and Abby
And for Luke, Alex and Helen

TABLE OF CONTENTS

CHAPTER 1
WELCOME TO
CANDLESTONE INN!

Birds! That's what I hear, Nikki Taylor-Michaelson realized as she opened her eyes sleepily to a bubbly high-pitched sound. Birds!

Wide awake now, she jumped out of bed and ran to the window of her new room. She'd been too sleepy the night before to examine it except for noticing that most of her belongings were already there. The only other things she'd really seen were the toolshed and the barn in the backyard, plus the huge upright stone that rose like a giant candle nearby. The barn would be perfect for housing the stray or wounded animals that Nikki was sure she'd find now that she and her family had moved to the country.

Nikki pulled up the shade and looked eagerly out over a green lawn that sloped gently to a small pond and then rose to rolling distant hills. Here and there on the lawn were blossoming apple trees and stately birches. And on the newly leafed-out branches of a twisted oak were what appeared to be hundreds of blackbirds, twittering against a cloudy sky.

Wow, Nikki thought, turning away and reaching for her jeans. What a racket!

Still, it was a lot better than the screeching brakes and wailing sirens she'd gotten used to hearing back home in Boston.

But Bennet, Vermont, is home now, she told herself, retrieving yesterday's T-shirt from the floor next to her bed. I live at the Candlestone Inn, named for that tall rock out back. And I'm an innkeeper's daughter, she thought, giggling.

"Nikki! Breakfast!"

That was Mom. "Coming!" Nikki called.

"Give Travis a shake on your way."

And that was Louise, Mom's partner in the inn and in life. She was Nikki and Travis's other mom since she'd adopted them both when they were babies, soon after Mom had.

"Okay," Nikki called back. Pulling on her battered Nikes and giving her short blond curls a shake rather than a brushing, she ran down the narrow upstairs hall to her brother's room.

There were four rooms plus a bathroom in the "family wing" of the inn's third floor: Nikki's, Travis's, Mom and Louise's, and a storage room. Nikki hadn't seen any of them clearly last night when they'd arrived, tired and grumpy after many hours on the road from Boston. The adult Taylor-Michaelsons had bought the inn in the early spring, and had spent a lot of time there after that, supervising repairs and doing some themselves, while Nikki and Travis finished out the school year staying with friends. The trip from Boston, which took just about a whole day, was too long for them to join their parents in Bennet on weekends. Staying with friends had been fun, but it was great to be together as a family again. It would be fun, too, having Mom and Louise home all the time. They'd both left jobs in Boston, Mom as a tax accountant and Louise as a computer programmer, as soon as they'd saved enough money to buy the inn. "Now we can do what we've always wanted," Mom had explained to Nikki and Travis, "if we all pull together to make it work."

That, thought Nikki, shouldn't be too hard. Mom, who one of their friends called "Mrs. Inside," would be in charge of the housekeeping. Louise, who the same friend called "Mrs. Outside," would be in charge of the grounds. And they'd all work on the remaining renovations.

"Travis!" Nikki yelled, pounding on his door and then flinging it open. "Breakfast!"

Travis was sitting on the edge of his bed, dressed and drawing on a large pad, his freckled nose wrinkled in concentration. Travis was always sketching scientific-looking diagrams. He wanted to be an inventor as firmly as Nikki wanted to be a veterinarian.

She flopped down beside him. "What's that?" she asked.

"Louise wants gardens, remember?" he said, still sketching. "And she said she'd have to have a fence for the vegetable one, because of deer and raccoons. So I'm working on designing the gate."

Nikki peered over his shoulder. "Cool. But don't you have to know what kind of fence she wants?"

"I do know, nosey." Travis stood up. "I smell bacon. Race you to the kitchen."

Nikki won. She was twelve, a year older than Travis, thinner and more athletic. Besides, she got ahead of him before they left his room, and there wasn't enough space in the narrow hall or on the narrower back stairs for him to pass.

Even so, they burst into the kitchen at nearly the same time — the back stairs led right into it — and Nikki nearly tripped over Max, their black Labrador retriever, who scrambled up to greet them. "Whoa, Maxie!" she said, hugging him to keep herself from falling. "Good morning. Hi, Snowball," she added, scooping the small white cat up from the chair she supposed would be hers.

Snowball gave her a disdainful look and jumped onto the counter where her food dish sat, safely away from Max.

"She's feeling put-upon," Mom said, flipping eggs. Her round face, framed with wispy brown curls, was flushed from the stove's heat. "I couldn't find her basket last night."

"I'll find it." Travis waved his drawing. "I think I've solved the gate problem."

Louise, her gardening clothes showing signs of freshly ground-in dirt, reached for the drawing with a hand that was also pretty grimy. Louise was taller than Mom, and not as round, with smile crinkles at the corners of her usually merry blue-green eyes. "Let's see," she said. "H'mm. That might just work. Only could it open the other way, Trav? Handle on the other side?"

Travis took the drawing back. "No problem. I always forget not everyone is left-handed."

Louise gave him a quick squeeze. "You're my favorite lefty." She went to the sink and washed her hands as Mom, lifting an egg from the pan, said, "Plates, please. And would someone get the bacon? It's staying warm in the oven."

After breakfast, and after they'd all done the dishes — they didn't have a dishwasher — Louise said, "Okay. Family conference. We've got only about twenty-four hours before the first guests arrive, and..."

"First guests!" Nikki exclaimed, excited at the prospect. "Who?"

Mom glanced at Louise and grinned. "Several people. We've got reservations for all but one room. Well, all but three if you count the two finished ones on the third floor, but we've decided not to rent those till the rest of the third floor's ready. As Louise said, we've got only twenty-four hours to make sure everything's in perfect shape. Thank goodness Louise and I were able to move most of our stuff up last week. But we still need time..."

"...time to make sure that we know what we're doing," Louise said, finishing Mom's sentence as she often did.

"Rules first, I'm afraid," said Mom.

"Protest now," Louise told them, "if you

think any of them are unfair."

"Okay." Nikki tapped Travis's sketch pad. "You might listen, Trav," she said.

"First rule," Mom began, giving Nikki a look. "No spats in front of the guests."

"We're not in front of them now," Nikki said. "Travis!"

"Sorry." Travis put the pad down. "I just couldn't get the shading right. Sorry."

"Second rule," Louise continued. "No going into the public areas without permission or without a definite task."

"What about Max and Snowball?" Nikki asked.

"That applies to them, too," Mom told her. "At least until we see how they behave."

"Inns should have dogs," Nikki said.

"I like the idea of an inn dog, too," said Louise, "but not everyone likes dogs, and Max can get pretty rambunctious, especially when he's been in swimming..."

"...which he's bound to do," Mom added, "given the pond. Now, look. The back of the house is ours — this kitchen, the bathroom and sitting room off it, plus the back porch..."

"...and the back part of the third floor," Louise finished.

"What about the back part of the second floor?" asked Nikki. "The back stairs go through there on their way to the back part of the third floor."

"Yes, but the whole second floor's for guests. We'll keep the second-floor door to the stairs locked. The guests will use the front stairs and we can go right up to the third floor from the kitchen."

"The outbuildings are ours," said Louise. "The barn and the shed. And the gardens. There's going to be a lot of weeding to do."

Nikki groaned.

"Can I have some of the barn," asked Travis, "for my shop?"

"Louise?" asked Mom.

"Sure. And Nikki," Louise went on, as if she knew what Nikki was thinking, "you can have part of it for waifs and strays. I just need a biggish corner for tools and fertilizer and stuff."

"Since it *is* a barn," Nikki said hopefully, "how about a horse?"

Mom and Louise both sighed, and Louise gave Nikki's shoulder a pat. "Maybe someday. I'd like one, too, Nikki. But we can't swing it now. We've got to make the inn work first. Is that the doorbell?"

It was. But Louise called Nikki and Travis back when they attempted to go into the public part of the house with Mom. Travis was just muttering, "You'd think we could answer the door, at least. What if you guys aren't home?" when Mom came back with a man in khakis, who was wearing an official-looking badge.

"This is Sheriff Bates," Mom said, looking worried. "He wants to talk to all of us."

CHAPTER 2
UNSETTLING NEWS

"Good morning, everyone." The sheriff settled his large frame into the kitchen chair Louise pulled out for him. His cheeks hung loosely on each side of his face, reminding Nikki of a bulldog's jowls. "Nice place you've got here. Should do well. Good location for skiers in the winter and hikers and tourists in the summer."

"That's what we're hoping," Mom said. "Coffee?"

"Yes, thanks, ma'am, don't mind if I do. It looks to be a long day, and a little extra coffee never hurt." He winked at Travis. Nikki saw him wink back; Travis was always outwardly polite to strangers, but she knew that inwardly he was just as fascinated as she was with the sheriff's cheeks. The sheriff sucked them in a little as he raised the coffee mug to his lips. But he did seem nice.

"Fun for you kids, I bet," he said after a long swallow, "especially when people bring their kids to stay. You're pretty isolated out here."

"Yes." Louise poured herself more coffee. "I guess our nearest neighbors are the two men who run the restaurant at the bottom of the hill."

The sheriff nodded. "The Fox and Hare," he said. "Yes. That'll be Charley Baxter and Don Evans. Nice fellows. Pity they never married." He winked again, this time at Louise.

"So, Sheriff," Mom said. "You mentioned you had something to tell us?"

The sheriff put down his mug. "Yes, ma'am. Mind you, I wouldn't want you to worry, but I've got to notify everyone in this area, especially folks who live out of the town center, like you do. And you might be especially at risk, being as how you take in strangers and all."

"At risk?" Nikki leaned forward. That sounded more exciting than alarming; how much risk could there be so far away from Boston? It was in cities that bad things happened — wasn't it?

Louise glanced at Mom; Mom raised her eyebrows. "Most of our guests," said Louise, "will have advance reservations. Not all, of course; we'll be advertising in the local paper..."

"We've already started," Mom put in. "We sent them an ad last week."

The sheriff nodded as if he approved. "I doubt you'll have much trouble anyway, but it does pay to be careful. 'Be prepared,' like the scouts say." He winked at Travis again, and Travis solemnly winked back. Then the sheriff dropped his voice. "It seems there's been an art heist," he said, "down in Boston. And it looks like the thief or thieves headed up this way."

"Wow!" Nikki exclaimed, and simultaneously, Travis asked, "What's a heist?"

"A theft." Louise put down her coffee mug, her merry eyes turning serious. "What was taken?"

"From where?" Mom asked.

"Who did it?" Nikki blurted out.

"If we knew that, missy," said the sheriff, "we'd have half the battle won. It looks like a pretty professional job," he went on. "No fingerprints, nothing careless. It was a special exhibit at the big art museum there. Egyptian stuff."

"Mummies?" Travis asked hopefully.

"In the exhibit, yes. But not in the heist. It'd be pretty hard to make off with a mummy, now wouldn't it, son?"

"Not if you dismembered it. And I've just figured out how to make a special box..."

"Travis," warned Mom. "Let the sheriff finish."

"Sorry." But under his breath, Travis muttered, "It's a pretty cool box."

"Only one thing was taken," said the sheriff. "A scarab. Valued at about half a million dollars, I think. They tell me it's perfect, not a flaw in it, and absolutely authentic."

"Wow!" said Nikki again. She knew from an Egyptian unit at school that scarabs were ancient beetles of some sort, and that they'd been considered sacred. She also knew Louise had a bracelet of little fake ones, all different colors. "What color?" she asked.

"Bright blue. Almost turquoise. The trouble is," the sheriff went on after downing the rest of his coffee, "the darn thing's so tiny it's easy to hide."

"How tiny?" asked Louise.

"Only about an inch long and half an inch wide." He pushed his chair back from the table and stood, his face very solemn. "And one of those travel maps, you know, from a computer, was found stuck between the scarab's case and a cat statue. The route from Boston to Bennet was clearly marked on it. So..."

"Hey!" Nikki exclaimed. "The thief could've been driving on the same road we were driving on!"

"There's no proof the map belonged to the thief," the sheriff said. "Still, we can't be sure it didn't. I just want to warn you that whoever's got the scarab is bound to be prepared to do anything to keep it and avoid capture. Just let me know if you see anything or anyone suspicious. With so many strangers coming and going — just keep your eyes open and be care-ful."

"What would anyone want with a scarab anyway?" Travis asked.

"Money, dork-face," Nikki said. "Half a million dollars."

"Right." The sheriff winked again. "Whoever's got it will probably try to contact someone else. The person who steals this sort of thing usually sells it to a dealer. A fence, we call it. The fence hangs onto it for a while and then sells it himself, once the heat's off. Anyway, again, with so many strangers coming to your inn — well, you never know who might turn up at a place like this. Like I said, keep your eyes open and be careful. Don't try any sleuthing yourselves." He looked sternly at Travis and Nikki. "You leave that to me. Just call me if you see anything suspicious."

"Like what, exactly?" Mom asked, standing up herself. "I mean, we can't very well go through all our guests' luggage or follow them around or anything like that."

"No, no, of course not. But you can be alert

to odd behavior — unexplained late night phone calls or meetings, that kind of thing. Well, folks," he said, going to the door to the main part of the inn. "Cheerio. Thanks for the coffee. Good luck with the inn."

"Would you like a quick tour?" Louise asked.

"No thanks," said the sheriff, "can't today. I've got to get going. There's a storm brewing, too, and wouldn't you know, I forgot my raincoat. Another time, maybe. But I'll be sure to recommend the inn to tourists. They sometimes stop in at the office and ask about places to stay. It's okay," he added, as Mom and Louise moved toward the door. "I'll see myself out." He glanced out the window over the sink. "Storm'll clear quickly, I think. Raining now, though. And there might even be a little thunder," he called as he lumbered out. "Mountain weather's unpredictable."

"Wow," said Nikki for the third time, after he'd left. "I bet this is just the kind of place the thief might come to. It'd be a good hideout. We'd better keep our eyes open, like he said."

"Collect clues," Travis suggested. "Write them down."

"Yeah, great," said Nikki. "But first we'd better find out more about scarabs. Can we use the computer?"

"Yes," said Mom. "Yes, you can use the computer, for a few minutes anyway. But please don't go online. We haven't got a second phone line yet and we need to keep the one we have open for inn business. And don't get carried away," she added. "The chances of the thief's coming here are pretty remote."

"But maybe they're not," said Travis. "The sheriff even said..."

"There are lots of other places to stay around here, Travis," Mom said. "Motels, other inns."

"And motels are a lot more impersonal," Louise added. "If I were an art thief, I'd go to a motel instead of an inn. Wouldn't you, Mindy?"

"I might. But what I don't understand is why the thief would come here at all. It should be easier to sell stolen goods in Boston than in northern Vermont."

"True," said Louise, "but remember what

the sheriff said about the map. If it was the thief's, that's a pretty good sign he was coming here."

"Or she," Nikki said. "Why does everyone think thieves are always men?"

Louise laughed. "You're right, pumpkin. Could be a woman."

"But we're not going to be suspicious of every guest," Mom said sternly. "It'd be awful to have us snooping around corners..." She darted out the kitchen door and peered around it, her eyes wide. "...looking people up and down suspiciously when they arrive..." She took two giant steps to Travis, pulled him to his feet, and scanned him, top to toe, frowning.

Louise laughed again, along with Travis and Nikki. "Right, Mindy. Good point. Actually, I think we should try to forget the whole thing."

"Not before we find out what we're looking for," Nikki said. "Come on, Travis." She grabbed his hand and pulled him to the door.

"We're not looking for it," Mom called after them. "We're just going to be alert to suspicious behavior."

But by then, as the rain increased outside, Nikki and Travis were halfway to the computer in the inn's wide and spacious front hall.

CHAPTER 3
UNEXPECTED COMPANY

The computer was on a big desk where Mom and Louise planned to register the guests and where Mom planned to keep the inn's business and financial records. Travis got there first and booted up while Nikki reached for the encyclopedia CD-ROM and slid it in. Travis typed in the keyword *scarab*.

"*Gem* or *Egypt*?" he asked when the screen showed two choices.

"Both, I guess," said Nikki. "Maybe *Gem* first, since the stolen one's supposed to be so valuable."

Travis clicked on *Gem*, and then he gave a low whistle as a long article came into view.

"Here's *Egypt*." Nikki ran her finger down the screen.

"*Starting in the ninth dynasty*," Travis read out loud, "*carved with symbols or designs or pictures. Faience*...what's that?"

"Some kind of stone, I think. I think those other things are. At least I know quartz is..."

"*Amethyst, carnelian, jasper*," Travis read. "Jasper's a boy's name, isn't it?"

"Is it? A girl can be called Ruby, so I guess a boy could be called Jasper."

Travis made a disapproving face. "How about granite? Granite Jones walked confidently up to the plate, swinging his bat..."

Nikki punched him lightly. "Be serious." She turned back to the screen. "Look. It says that scarabs aren't worth much as art objects but are important to history."

"Then why is the sheriff so upset? And why did he say this one was worth — how much did he say?"

"Half a million dollars." Nikki reached for

the mouse. "Look at all the other countries that had scarabs, too." She scrolled down. *"Greece: scarabs carved with gods and demons, and animals and archers. Etruria..."*

"But our scarab's Egyptian. At least the sheriff said it was stolen from an Egyptian exhibit."

"Right." Nikki touched Travis's forehead. "You actually do have a brain in there! Okay. Let's go back to *Egypt.*"

Travis took the mouse and moved up to *Egypt* again.

"Hey," he said delightedly, "it's got to do with mummies after all!"

Nikki read out loud. *"Scarabs were put on mummies to protect them. They were often carved to look like dung beetles."*

"Isn't dung manure?" Travis said. "Gross!"

Nikki glanced ahead. "They made rings out of them, too. Seal rings."

Travis barked like a seal and flapped his arms like flippers.

"Jerk! Not that kind of seal. You use a seal ring to seal a letter."

"Huh?"

"People did that in medieval times, I think," Nikki explained. "I guess they didn't have envelopes, or at least not envelopes with glue. You folded your paper over, dropped hot wax — sealing wax it was called — on it, and then when it was still soft, you pressed your ring in it. I guess it sort of worked like a return address, too. Each ring was different, so people could tell who'd sent the letter."

"Cool," said Travis. "Hey, maybe our scarab is a ring."

"Maybe. I guess it could be. And," she added, "it won't be hard to check people's hands for rings. We wouldn't have to go through their luggage or anything."

"If you'd just stolen a scarab ring," said Travis, "would you go around wearing it?" He removed the encyclopedia CD-ROM and shut down the computer. "I sure wouldn't. I'd hide it away in my luggage. You know," he said thoughtfully, "maybe I'll be a detective instead of an inventor."

"A vet," said Nikki, "is already a detective,

sort of, figuring out what's wrong with a sick animal who can't talk..."

"Nikki! Travis! Anyone want to go on a tour of the house while we still have it to ourselves?"

Travis nodded, so Nikki shouted, "Yes! Okay, Mom!" and followed him into the kitchen. They'd gone through the whole house briefly one long weekend right after Mom and Louise had bought it, but since going back and forth from Boston took most of any normal weekend, they hadn't visited again, and hadn't seen the renovations.

"As we said," Mom told them when they got to the kitchen, "none of us should wander around the public areas when guests are there, except to do specific jobs and to be available to answer questions. But we should all know the layout of the house, and which parts are open and which aren't."

"Let's start at the front door," Louise suggested, coming down the stairs in clean jeans and a clean rose-colored polo shirt. "And go on from there."

The front door led directly into the wide hall, with stairs leading up on one side. A door to the right of the front door led into a spacious living room, and an arch to the left led into the dining room, bright and cheerful, with many windows. The kitchen was beyond the dining room, its entrance a double door. There was a little interior window with shutters and a wide, shelf-like sill cut into the wall near the door; it opened into the kitchen. "The sill's for putting trays and plates on," Mom explained, "since we'll be serving breakfast. Guests will probably come to the window to ask for things, so we'll have to keep the kitchen nice and neat."

Snowball appeared on the sill.

"I hope our guests like cats," said Louise dryly. "I don't think we'll be able to keep her off the sill, Mindy."

Mom picked Snowball up and deposited her on the family side of the kitchen door. "I don't either," she said. "We'll just have to see how that goes."

"Where are we putting the TV?" Travis asked. "Our TV, I mean."

"In our sitting room," Mom answered, "off the kitchen."

"Can't we ever use the big living room?" asked Nikki.

"Maybe in the off-season," said Louise, "when we don't have any guests."

"Now," said Mom, "let me show you my favorite room." She led them back through the dining room into a small, cozy room behind the living room and next to the stairs. The walls were lined with bookcases, and several large, softly upholstered wing chairs were arranged in a semicircle in front of a huge stone fireplace. The fireplace was so deep a person could easily walk into it and stand up.

"The library," said Mom. "This is where I want to hang out in the winter when we don't have any guests and it's pouring rain or blizzarding outside."

"Me, too!" said Nikki.

"We'll have guests in the winter," Louise said. "Skiers."

"Yes," Mom agreed, "but not always. Not when it doesn't snow."

"It'll snow," said Louise, and Travis, who loved skiing as much as she did, said, "It better!"

"What's this?" Nikki pointed to a narrow door at one side of the fireplace.

"That's to the East Wing," Louise answered. "The part of the house we haven't finished working on yet."

"Off limits," Mom told them. "Some of it's torn up, floors and walls and things. It needs a lot more work."

"Can we see it?"

"Maybe another time, when it's safer," Louise said. "And maybe you can help us with it now that we'll be here all year 'round."

"But we need to make some money first," said Mom, "before we can afford to finish restoring it. Let's go upstairs now."

They went back to the front hall and climbed the wide staircase to the second floor.

That floor had several bathrooms, plus seven bedrooms, each a different color: the deep blue room, the pale blue room, the green room, the lavender room, the yellow room, the white room, the pink room. On the third floor, separate from the family's sleeping quarters, there were more bathrooms and five more bedrooms in the closed-off East Wing. "Bedrooms-in-progress," Louise called them. "Those are the ones we'll be working on next."

"Right," said Mom. "Who wants to learn how to wallpaper?"

Travis shook his head and Nikki said doubtfully, "Maybe. I'd rather do carpentry or plastering or..."

She was interrupted by a sudden clap of thunder. Max began barking frantically.

"There's the thunder the sheriff mentioned," said Louise. "I'm glad I put the garden tools away."

Max barked again. Mom frowned and said, "He's not usually bothered by storms."

"No, he's not," said Louise. "Maybe someone's coming."

Mom looked alarmed. "It can't be a guest so soon! At least not one with a reservation."

"I'll go!" Travis ran to the stairs. Nikki ran after him and Mom and Louise followed more sedately.

When Travis opened the door, a young bearded man, wearing hiking boots, a sodden green shirt and jeans, and an equally sodden day pack over one shoulder, stumbled in.

"Oh, please," he said, his voice thick and desperate. "I need..."

But before he could say any more, the pack slid off his shoulder and he fell in a soaking wet heap onto the floor.

CHAPTER 4
THE STRANGER

For a moment they all stared at the fallen man. Then Mom exclaimed, "Oh, my word!" Louise said, "911," and ran for the phone. Nikki said, "He's soaking wet," and Travis shouted, "There's someone else coming!"

Sure enough, outside, two men in raincoats had gotten out of an old-fashioned wood-sided station wagon and were now walking up the flagstone path to the inn's front door. One of them was short and somewhat stubby, but jolly looking, with twinkling brown eyes and a wide smile. The other was taller, with a black beard flecked with gray; he seemed somewhat solemn and formal, but just as friendly.

"Hello there," the short one said to Nikki and Travis as both men stepped up to the open door. "We're the welcoming committee, Charley and Don, from the restaurant down the road. I'm Charley and he's Don. And you must be Nikki and Travis Taylor-Michaelson. We've already met your moms, and... Merciful heavens, who's this?" Charley stared down at the man at their feet.

Louise came running back from the phone. "There's no 911 here," she gasped. "Can you believe that? So I called the police and the dispatcher said the ambulance is out on another call. She said it's the fire department number, really, that one should call for an ambulance..."

"Dr. Pix," said Charley, striding to the phone. "May I?" he called over his shoulder.

"Yes, of course," Mom called back. "Thank you!"

"He's our doctor," the taller man, Don, explained. "Shouldn't we get this poor fellow inside?"

"Yes," Louise said. "We certainly should!"

"Is there a sofa?" Don asked. "Charley and I can carry him."

"There's one in the living room," Nikki told him. The fallen man, she could see, was very pale and didn't seem to be moving at all. As she studied him, noticing his wet, rumpled clothes and the dark stubble on his cheeks and chin, it suddenly hit her that he might have something to do with the stolen scarab. If anyone could be a fugitive, he could!

"You might not want him in the public living room," Don said. "If you're expecting guests."

"Yeah," Travis whispered to Nikki. "How would you feel if you arrived at an inn and saw an unconscious body in the living room?"

"The sitting room sofa, then," said Nikki. "Off the kitchen."

"Perfect!" Louise patted Nikki's shoulder.

"Doctor's on his way," Charley said, coming back.

Don gestured to Charley, who bent down and seized the prone man's shoulders. Don took his feet, and the Taylor-Michaelsons led them into the kitchen. Max barked and Snowball scurried under the table as soon as they got there.

"No, Max," Nikki said severely when the dog jumped up, tail wagging and tongue lolling, as Charley and Don gently laid the man on the sofa. "He's very friendly," she explained.

"I can see that." Charley grunted a little; his face had turned quite red. He gave Max a pat. "Nice dog. Labrador?"

"Yes," said Travis. "You like dogs?"

"Love 'em." Charley scratched Max behind the ears, and Max gave a quiet, ecstatic moan. "In fact, I think I must have been a dog in my first life."

"That's why Charley does the cooking and I greet the guests," Don said, his face still serious. By the time Nikki realized that what he'd said was a joke, he'd finished undoing the man's shirt buttons and was saying, "Here, Charley, just help me get this off."

"Actually," said Louise, "shouldn't we get all his wet things off? And your coats, too," she added. "Let me take them."

"Thank you." Don shrugged out of his wet raincoat; Charley did the same, and handed both coats to Louise, who hung them over chairs.

"Now," Charley said briskly, "got any extra blankets?"

"Yes," said Mom. "Children, just run up to the linen closet and get some, would you?"

"What linen closet?" Nikki asked.

"It's on the second floor landing," Louise told her. "You can't miss it. Big white door. We've only just finished showing the kids around the house," she explained to Charley and Don. "We didn't get to fine points like closets."

"I see." Don turned back to the stranger as Nikki and Travis moved reluctantly toward the kitchen door. "Now then. I think our friend will need something dry to wear. I don't suppose you've got any men's pajamas or anything?"

"Nothing that would fit him," Mom said.

"I'll just scoot back home and get a pair of yours," said Charley. "It's obvious mine would be too big, isn't it?" he added when Don gave him a funny look.

"Children," Mom said as if she'd just noticed they were still there, "the blankets!"

In no time, the strange man — who, it turned out, had a bloody bump on the back of his head — was firmly installed on the sitting room sofa, wearing a pair of red and white pajamas and a tan chamois shirt of Don's, plus a pair of ski socks of Louise's. Mom had wrapped him in several of the inn's extra blankets, too. As thunder continued to rumble outside, Don and Charley sat at the kitchen table with the Taylor-Michaelsons, the adults with coffee and Nikki and Travis with cocoa. Max was lying next to the sofa, glancing anxiously up at the man every now and then, and Snowball was curled up on the man's stomach.

"I hope he likes cats," Nikki said.

"Yeah, it'd be tough if he suddenly started sneezing or something," said Travis. "A-choo!

A-choo! There was this kid in my class..."

"I wonder who he is," said Mom.

"Billy Pargiter," Travis said, and Nikki kicked him under the table. "Mom means the man, you dork," she whispered loudly.

"I imagine he'll tell us who he is when he wakes up," Don said. "I wouldn't bother him now, he seems so peaceful. There wasn't much in his pockets. No wallet, even."

"That's odd," said Mom. "Isn't it? I mean, most people carry wallets, at least."

Don looked at his watch. "Dr. Pix should be here by now."

"The storm might've slowed him down a bit," Charley said. "Still, I'll call his beeper if he's not here soon." He cleared his throat. "Well," he said heartily, as if trying to cheer them all up. "Why don't we get on with the original purpose of our visit..."

"...which was to welcome you," Don said.

"And," Charley finished with a flourish, "to invite you to come have dinner tonight at the restaurant."

"Oh, but we..." Mom began, but Don interrupted.

"A free meal, you understand," he said. "A welcome-to-our-community meal. Don't worry, after that, we'll charge."

"Well," said Charley. "*Maybe* we'll charge. But not for special occasions. After all," he said to Don, "they *are* neighbors. And with the inn right up the road..."

"We'll probably be sending you business," Mom said, smiling, but Nikki could see that she was keeping a wary eye on the hiker, although he certainly didn't look as if he was going to move any time soon.

Charley smiled back. "If you like my cooking. And we'll probably be sending you business."

"If you like our rooms." Mom stood up. "We'll give you a tour" — she gestured toward the unconscious man — "later."

"That would be wonderful," Don said politely.

Charley looked toward the sitting room. "You must've broken through a wall to make that archway into the sitting room where the sofa is.

Wasn't this originally two smallish rooms?"

"Yes," Louise told him. "But they were kind of dark and since they're going to be our main daytime living quarters, we thought we'd open them up a bit. We ran into trouble, though, when we..."

As Louise launched into a detailed description of the renovations, punctuated with contributions from Mom, Nikki and Travis drifted into the sitting room and looked down at the unconscious man.

"I wish we knew who he is," Travis said.

Nikki decided to keep her suspicions to herself, so she just said, "Yeah, so do I."

"Suppose he doesn't wake up?" Travis asked nervously.

"He will. At least," Nikki said, looking nervously at him herself, "he probably will sometime."

Travis went over to the sofa and peered into the man's face. "He doesn't look too good. And he's breathing funny."

Nikki joined him in watching the man's chest. It did go up and down, but not very often or very much. Still, he was clearly alive. "I think he's okay," she said. "You don't breathe much when you're asleep, after all."

"Yes, you do. You breathe a lot. Slowly but deeply. Haven't you ever seen anyone sleeping?"

"I've seen you," Nikki retorted. "You snore."

"I do not!" Travis exclaimed indignantly. Just as he did, the man stirred and moaned.

Both Nikki and Travis froze.

Nikki bent closer. "Hello?" she said softly.

No response.

"Sir?" she said, a little closer and a little louder. "Mister?"

Travis pushed her aside. "Hi, there," he said in a loud voice. "Welcome to Candlestone Inn."

The man moaned again.

"Welcome to Candlestone Inn!" Travis shouted directly into his ear.

The man opened his eyes and stared at them blankly. "H-h-hello," he said vaguely. "Who are you? Where am I? What...?" He struggled to sit up.

Snowball leapt off the man's stomach and

Max put his front paws on the sofa and licked his face.

"Hey, Max, I don't think you'd better do that." Nikki moved the dog away. "And I really don't think you ought to sit up," she said to the man. "You've got a bad bump on your head; the doctor's coming. You probably shouldn't move."

"Oh." The man scanned the room anxiously. "I — I see. Okay." He lay back on the sofa, and explored the back of his head gingerly with his hand. "My head does hurt. Have you got any aspirin?"

"Sure," Travis told him.

But as Travis started to leave, Nikki held him back. "Maybe you shouldn't take anything," she told the man, "at least till the doctor's seen you."

"Okay," the man said again. He seemed quite young, and very willing to please. Gentle, Nikki thought. Not like a robber at all.

"I'm Nikki Taylor-Michaelson," she said, "and this is my brother Travis. That cat who was sitting on you till you moved is Snowball, and the dog who licked you is Max. He's very friendly. So's Snowball..."

"I hope you like cats and dogs," Travis said. "I hope you're not allergic or anything."

"I — I don't know," the man said. "Where...? Who...?"

"This is the Candlestone Inn," Nikki explained. "Our moms run it, Mindy and Louise Taylor-Michaelson. They're just in there, talking." She pointed into the kitchen, where Mom and Louise were still enthusiastically describing the renovations to Charley and Don, with occasional glances toward the sitting room. They had the architect's plans out now, and were bent over them intently.

"Your — your moms?" The man looked confused.

"That's right. They both adopted us. We used to live in Boston. Our moms bought the inn and fixed it up. We've just moved in, and we open tomorrow. Lots of people will be arriving then."

"I see," the man said. "Lots of people? But why? Where?"

Nikki glanced at Travis and saw that he was beginning to think the same thing she was: that the bump on the man's head had somehow addled his brain. "What's your name?" she asked gently. "Is there anyone we should notify?"

"My — name? Notify?" The man frowned and pursed his lips, as if trying to remember. "I don't know," he said, sounding surprised.

"Your wife?" Travis suggested. "Or maybe your girlfriend, or mother? Or a friend? Were you hiking with someone? You were wearing hiking boots." He pointed to them; they were on the floor beside the sofa.

"Was I?"

"And," Nikki exclaimed, suddenly remembering, "you had a day pack." She dashed out, found it under a table near the front door, brought it back, and held it up to the man.

The man struggled again to sit and succeeded this time. He still looked so bewildered Nikki was sure there was something seriously wrong with his memory. "Is that mine?" he asked softly, looking at the pack.

Travis gave Nikki a glance. "You were carrying it. That kind of makes it look that way."

"Oh." The man rubbed his forehead, then fingered the bump again. "Yes, I guess it does."

Out of the corner of her eye, Nikki saw the adults move to the sink, where Louise seemed to be pointing out something about the pipes. Nikki knelt beside the sofa. "Mister," she said as calmly as she could, "do you remember your name?"

"My — name," he said. "I — I think..." Then with a look of utter astonishment, he said, "No. No, I don't remember my name." Suddenly he buried his face in his hands and fell back on the sofa, groaning. "Oh, my God!" he said. "I don't know who I am! I don't know who I am!"

Nikki put her hand on his arm, stroking it gently. "Never mind," she said. "It's probably just temporary. I think bumps on the head can do that, can make you forget. The doctor'll be here soon. Just rest. Don't think about it."

"The pack," Travis said. "Maybe there's something in the pack, a wallet or something. Maybe your name's in there somewhere."

With a sudden burst of energy, the man sat

up again. "Yes," he said eagerly. "Oh, yes. Let's look!"

Travis picked up the pack and opened it.

And there, right on top, nestled in cotton in a camper's aluminum drinking cup, was a bright turquoise scarab.

CHAPTER 5
WHO IS HE?

C arefully, even though it didn't look as if it could possibly break, Nikki lifted the scarab up and showed it to the still-unidentified man.

"Good heavens," said Mom, coming into the room with the other adults. "Isn't that...?" She glanced at Louise and they both moved closer to Nikki and Travis.

Nikki watched the man carefully, suspicious now instead of sympathetic. But he appeared to be so completely bewildered and so distressed at having six people staring at him that she became sympathetic again almost immediately.

She was sure even before he spoke that he didn't know anything about it.

"What — what's that?" he asked.

"You tell us," Travis said severely. Nikki kicked him and he kicked her back.

"I have no idea." The man rubbed his head again. "It looks like one of those Egyptian things, a — what's it called? Carob — no, that's not it — satrap — no, that's something else. Oh," he moaned, "can't I even *think*?"

"Scarab." Travis stared sternly into the man's eyes as if he were pretending to be a police officer questioning a suspect. "There's one missing from a big museum down in Boston."

"There is?" said Charley.

Louise and Mom drew Charley and Don aside, filling them in on what the sheriff had told them. Louise, Nikki could see, was keeping a wary eye on the man as they talked.

"But I don't know anything about..." the man cried defensively. "Oh, no!" He leaned back, looking so distressed Nikki was afraid he might burst out crying any minute. "Really. I have no idea how it got there, and I didn't know one was missing, or anything. Or even who I am. It's..."

Nikki put her hand on his arm again. "It'll be okay," she said soothingly, shooting Travis a black look. "You'll see. It's probably some kind of mistake. Maybe this isn't even the missing scarab..."

"Oh, it's the missing one all right." Travis was still eyeing the man suspiciously. "I mean how many turquoise scarabs are there running around in the state of Vermont?"

Don came back to the sofa with the others and looked — rather sternly, Nikki thought — down at the man. "What's the last thing you remember?" he asked.

The man frowned. "I remember — I remember waking up," he told them, "and rolling up my sleeping bag..."

"Sleeping bag!" Nikki exclaimed. "But you didn't have one when you got here!"

"See?" Travis hissed.

Nikki stepped on Travis's foot, and ignored his indignant cry of, "Ouch! Cut that out!"

"So you must have had one of those big frame things," Charley said, "for your sleeping bag and cooking stuff." He seemed much friendlier toward the man than Don did.

"I must've," the man agreed. But he still looked bewildered.

"Maybe someone took that stuff," Nikki said, ignoring Travis. "And hit you over the head."

Louise put her hands on Nikki's shoulders and Mom moved closer to Travis. But they both now seemed to be sorry for the man.

The man frowned again. "I suppose that could be true. But I don't remember it."

"So is waking up the last thing you remember?" Don asked.

"Yes. No, wait. I woke up," the man said slowly, as if checking off items on a list. "I rolled up my sleeping bag — no. I got dressed. I rolled up my pajamas. I always wear pajamas even when I'm backpacking..." He looked around at all of them. "That says something, doesn't it? That I know I've done some back-packing, and that I know I wear pajamas. How odd!" he exclaimed. "Don't most backpackers sleep in their clothes or their underwear or something?"

"Probably," said Nikki. "I don't know. We've camped, but not backpacked. We always take pajamas."

"Not everyone does," Louise said.

"But backpacking's different," the man said eagerly, talking in a rush now. "You're carrying this huge pack, on a frame, with your sleeping bag and your tent, and you've got cooking stuff hanging from it, aluminum pots and pans and a drinking cup and..."

"Then where is all that stuff?" asked Travis. "All you had was this little day pack. And the scarab was in it in a drinking cup." He held the cup up. "Aluminum, too. So would you really have had all that other stuff?"

The man seemed bewildered again. "I don't know."

"Any more memories?" Mom asked gently. "You put your pjs in the sleeping bag, and then rolled it up..."

"And then I walked a while, I think. And

then — no, sorry. I don't remember anything else."

"Nothing?" asked Don.

"Not even a noise?" Charley suggested. "Footsteps, someone breathing?"

"No." The man shut his eyes for a minute as if trying to recreate the scene in his mind. "No. Nothing. Except..."

"Yes?" Nikki prompted eagerly. "What?"

"I'm not sure. But when I closed my eyes just then and tried to pretend I was back there, I thought I heard a sort of a bang, like — like a car door."

"So," Nikki said excitedly, "you must have been near a road..."

"Or a parking lot," Travis put in, seeming a little less skeptical now. "Do you remember anything else about where you were?"

"Not really. Trees..."

"What kind?" Don asked quickly.

"Don't know. Wait, I remember something scratchy, like pine needles, on the ground. At least I think I do. I'm not sure."

Louise sighed. "I'm afraid that could be any-place. Anything else?"

"Campsites, maybe? Water?" asked Travis.

"Good, Trav," Nikki said.

Travis stuck his tongue out at her.

"No other campsites," the man said with great certainty. "I never camp in camp-grounds... Wow! I guess that's another thing I know about myself. You folks are great!"

"Water," Travis suggested. "Especially if you don't go to campgrounds, you must camp where there's water."

"Or carry it in," Nikki said.

"Water's pretty heavy," Louise pointed out.

The man closed his eyes again. "I don't think I remember water. Maybe a brook. Maybe. I'm not sure."

"Then," said Don, "you must have carried water purification tablets. Do you remember that?"

"No." The man rubbed his head again. "I'm sorry. I don't feel..."

"You rest," Mom said soothingly, the way she spoke to Nikki and Travis and Louise when they were sick. "The doctor'll be here soon, I'm sure. Come on, everyone." She herded them all toward the archway leading into the kitchen.

"What about the you-know-what?" Travis whispered, holding back as the man closed his eyes and lay back down. "The scarab? We can't just leave it there."

Nikki hesitated. "No, I guess not. But I don't think we should touch it."

"You already did," Travis pointed out accusingly. "Your fingerprints are all over it. Dope!"

"We'll leave it right where it is," Louise said, pushing them ahead of her into the kitchen. "And we'll call that sheriff."

"There's the doorbell," Travis said unnecessarily as it rang.

"Good," Louise said. "It's probably the doctor."

It was the doctor, full of apologies for dripping water on the hall rug and for taking so long. Lightning, he said, had struck a tree, toppling it across the road during the worst part of the storm, and he'd had to wait for a road crew to clear it.

After he'd examined the injured hiker, as they'd all started calling him, the doctor reported that he'd had not one but two nasty blows on the head; he ordered the ambulance, which had returned from its earlier call, to remove the hiker to the hospital for observation. "We'll come see you!" Nikki called as the ambulance attendants wheeled him out, and the hiker waved weakly. His pack was beside him on the stretcher, minus the scarab, which the sheriff had removed when he'd arrived. He was going to send it to Boston, he told them, to make sure it was the right one. "If it is," he said, "we'll have to figure out if that fellow's telling the truth about never seeing it before. If he *is* telling the truth, I suppose the real thief could have planted it on him to throw suspicion off himself. I wonder when he was planning to take it back, though."

So now we have to wait and see what the museum people say, Nikki decided. "Still," she said to Travis quietly after the sheriff had left, "it won't hurt for us to go on keeping our eyes open anyway, in case it turns out to be the right scarab and the hiker isn't the thief."

"How many scarabs can there be?" Travis grumbled. But he agreed about keeping their eyes open.

The hiker could be faking, Nikki thought later, reluctantly changing into her best summer pants and a flowered vest for their dinner at The Fox and Hare. Mom had insisted that they all dress up. "We're new here," she'd said, "and we've got to remember we're running a business. It won't hurt us to be careful how we dress now and then, especially in public. We don't want to make a bad impression."

"I sure hope we're not going to have to dress up when we're home," Travis muttered, but Mom ignored him.

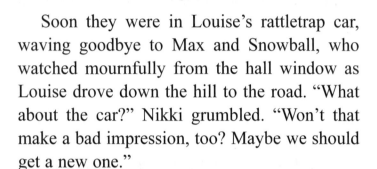

Soon they were in Louise's rattletrap car, waving goodbye to Max and Snowball, who watched mournfully from the hall window as Louise drove down the hill to the road. "What about the car?" Nikki grumbled. "Won't that make a bad impression, too? Maybe we should get a new one."

"We can't afford a new one yet," Louise said cheerfully. "And we're not going to drive the car into the restaurant."

The road to the restaurant was bumpy and winding — full of puddles, too, though the storm had stopped. It was parallel to the little town's main street and led off into the foothills of the same mountains that the Taylor-Michaelsons could see in the distance from the inn's hilltop seat. Thick woods rose on either side of the road, and they passed only one other car on the two-mile drive.

"I don't see how anyone finds this place," Louise said as they piled out of the car in front of the attractive brown-shingled building that housed The Fox and Hare. The red trim around the doors, the windows, and the wide front porch brightened the brown and gave the place a cozy country look. So did the ivy that climbed up either side of the front door and draped over the portico.

"But they do find it," Mom said, nodding back toward the parking lot, which was nearly full.

Inside, small pierced-tin lanterns shed amber light over the rough wooden tables and chintz-padded wooden chairs. A fireplace glowed at one end of the large main dining room, taking the edge off the chilly June evening. There was a pleasant buzz of conversation, punctuated by the clink of glasses and of silverware on china.

"I wish he'd loosen up," Travis muttered as they followed Don to a corner table.

"I think he's cool," said Nikki. "Elegant."

"We'll see." Travis sounded doubtful.

Nikki ordered roast chicken, and Travis ordered chopped sirloin, which Louise said was hamburger. "That's what I want," he said, still grumbling.

"There won't be a bun," Nikki warned him.

But Don, who was waiting on them and being the maitre d' and greeting customers at the door, said, "I suspect Charley can locate a bun and some ketchup. Fries, too?"

Travis looked happy for the first time that evening.

After they'd eaten and many of the other guests had left, Charley came out of the kitchen in his apron and chef's hat, bearing a tray that held a cake with a circle of lighted candles around its top edge. "It's not anyone's birthday," Travis pointed out.

"It's not a birthday cake," Charley said, beaming. "It's a welcome-to-Bennet cake. See?"

Written around the sides of the cake in blue icing were those words, and, on its top, "Best of luck to Candlestone Inn." In the middle of the cake was a small gray replica of the stone that had given the inn its name.

"Wow!" Travis breathed, and Mom and Louise beamed back at Charley. "That's wonderful!" Mom said.

"How did you do it?" asked Louise.

"When's more like it," Mom said. "That must've taken ages."

"It's his hobby." Don joined them, smiling fondly at Charley. "He's won several prizes. If you need a cake for any occasion, just ask."

"It's beautiful," said Mom. "Thank you."

"You're welcome," Charley said. "It was fun. Now," he went on, "anyone want ice cream to go with it? Vanilla, chocolate, strawberry, chocolate chip, mocha, fudge royale, peppermint."

"Peppermint," said Nikki quickly. "Please."

Travis had chocolate, as did Louise, and Mom had mocha. It was a very full Taylor-Michaelson family that waddled back out to the parking lot.

"It's been a busy day," Louise remarked, sighing as she unlocked the car.

"And tomorrow," said Mom, holding her seat back so Nikki and Travis could climb in, "comes our first official guest. Goodness, what's this?" She leaned around and pulled a piece of paper out from under the windshield wiper.

MIND YOUR OWN BUSINESS, it said in big black letters, IF YOU KNOW WHAT'S GOOD FOR YOU.

CHAPTER 6
THE FIRST GUESTS

With a rather sick smile, Louise looked at the note over Mom's shoulder. "It must be a mistake."

Mom looked grim. "I doubt it," she said.

"A prank," Louise insisted. "Someone mistook our car for someone else's. Oh, come on, Mindy, let's not spoil a nice evening — our last one before we have to worry about towels and sheets and morning muffins."

Mom smiled thinly and got into the car.

"I think Mom is right," Nikki whispered to Travis.

"Me, too," he whispered back. "There's too many weird things going on."

Nikki nodded, and later, after they'd all gone to bed and the house was quiet, she took an almost unused notebook out of the semi-unpacked box by her desk, slipped into Travis's room and sat crosslegged on the foot of his bed. "Okay," she said. "I guess we'd better start writing clues down. What've we got so far?"

"The stolen scarab," Travis said promptly. "That was the first thing."

Nikki wrote:

STOLEN SCARAB

in big letters.

Travis scooted to Nikki's end of the bed and peered over her shoulder. "You'd better put more than that. Here." He took the notebook from her, added TURQUOISE between STOLEN and SCARAB, and went on:

1. Stolen from Boston art museum
2. Considered valuable

"Good," Nikki said. "Then the man."
A few minutes later, they had:

STOLEN TURQUOISE SCARAB

    1. Stolen from Boston art museum

    2. Considered valuable

MYSTERIOUS HIKER

    1. Lost; head wounds; amnesia

    2. Turquoise scarab in pack

    3. Doesn't remember what happened

    4. Faking?

NOTE ON CAR

    1. "Mind your own business"

    2. Threat?

    3. Connection to theft?

"It's not much, really, is it?" said Nikki.

"No." Travis yawned. "But it's a start."

"The thing is," said Nikki, "that note on the car makes it look as if someone's trying to get us to ignore everything. And that must mean they have something to do with it, and are afraid we'll find out."

"Yeah, but why us?"

"I don't know. Because of the inn? Because the hiker came to us? Maybe he even put the note on the car."

"But he's in the hospital," Travis protested. "And he doesn't know anything about the scarab."

"That's what he said," Nikki said darkly. "Look, I liked him, too, but I think we have to be suspicious of everyone. You know Mom and Louise won't be."

"No," Travis agreed. "At least Louise won't. She likes everyone, and Mom almost does. But Mom's more careful of things. More suspicious, sort of."

Nikki snapped the notebook shut. "Still, we've got to protect them."

"You know," Travis said dubiously, "on second thought, if I were the thief, I think I'd just take off someplace."

"But this is someplace."

Travis stared at her. "Yes, Nikki," he said

kindly, "it is. Every place is someplace, my dear."

"Oh, shut up, Trav. That's not what I meant. Remember," she said, slowly, as if talking to a very young child, "what the sheriff said about that map with the route from Boston to Bennet marked on it."

"Yeah, okay," Travis said. "You're right." He yawned again. "So what we've got to do is check out all the guests pretty carefully. Especially any that have come here from Boston."

"Or even just through it," Nikki said. "We'd better start tomorrow."

There was no sign of rain the next morning. The doorbell rang very early, while the Taylor-Michaelsons were still having breakfast. "It's too early for the first guest, surely," Mom said, looking alarmed.

Louise nodded, but started to get up just as Nikki jammed her last bite of toast into her mouth and ran for the door, nearly tripping over Snowball and then over Travis, who'd caught up to her.

It was the sheriff.

"Just wanted to let you folks know," he said when they'd led him into the kitchen, "that the scarab's already back in the museum. We should hear soon if it's the stolen one. But I think we can probably consider that part of the case closed. The rest of it, too, I'll wager. That boy still says he doesn't remember who he is, but we'll clear that up right enough with a lie detector test."

"So you really do think the hiker stole it?" asked Mom, while Louise poured the sheriff a cup of coffee.

"But he seemed so nice!" Louise exclaimed.

"Nice is as nice does," the sheriff said. "Thanks. No, no sugar. Yes, I do think he stole it. It was in his pack, after all."

"But what about the bumps on his head?" Louise asked.

"Coincidence, maybe. He didn't have a wallet on him. Someone probably robbed him. Or maybe he never had one — didn't want to be identified."

"Mom," Travis said in a loud whisper. "The note?"

"Huh?" said the sheriff. "What note?"

"We found a note on our car last night," Nikki told him.

"Oh? Where? What did it say?"

Mom produced the note and showed it to the sheriff.

"It's probably just a prank," Louise said. "Scare the new people. Something like that."

The sheriff pocketed the note. "As you say, it could be a prank. But it also might not be. I'd like to hold onto it, just in case we need it. I doubt there's a connection, though. Let me know if anything else turns up, but don't lose sleep over it. You've got an inn to run — and," he added, looking out the window and then winking, "unless I miss my guess, you've got a customer coming up your driveway. I'll just be off. Thanks for the coffee. I'll go out the back, shall I, so I don't scare a paying guest."

"Thank you," Mom said nervously.

"What difference did that make?" Travis said as Louise whisked the breakfast dishes into the sink. "His car's out there big as life with SHERIFF written all over the door."

"Well, it was a nice gesture. Holy smoke!" Mom exclaimed as the doorbell rang. Max barked and Snowball ran under the sitting room sofa. "It's really happening!"

Louise gave her a little pat on the shoulder. "Yup. Mindy and Louise Taylor-Michaelson, innkeepers. Nikki and Travis Taylor-Michaelson, assistant innkeepers. Come on, family, time to go to work!"

And they all surged eagerly to the front door, each shouting, "Max, stay!" as they went.

"Let's not scare them to death," Mom whispered, "by meeting them in a huge pack. They're probably already wondering why the sheriff was here."

"No." Travis was looking out one of the small side windows bordering the door.

"They're talking with him. Smiling. One of them laughed."

"Let me see." Nikki pushed Travis aside.

"Mom's right," said Louise. "Nikki, you answer the door. Mindy, why don't you sit at the desk? Travis, you and I better go into the kitchen. We can come out when they're in. I'll show them to their room and you can bring up their luggage. Okay?"

"Okay," Mom said breathlessly. "Places, everyone!" She gave Nikki a little poke and went to the registration desk. "Wait'll they ring again, Nik," she said as Nikki reached for the doorknob.

They rang almost immediately.

Nikki yanked the door open more abruptly than she meant to, and put on her best smile. "Hello! Welcome to Candlestone Inn."

"Why, thank you, dear," said a short, stout woman in a flowered dress. "What a very lovely spot, isn't it, Herbert?" She turned to the cheerful-looking middle-aged man behind her.

Nikki tried not to stare at his red and green plaid pants, which clashed with his bright blue shirt and were tucked lumpily into black rubber boots — or at the small, round boy who suddenly emerged from behind the rhododendrons clustered near the inn's front door.

"Thank you," Nikki said demurely. "Please come in." She ushered them inside. "I'm Nikki Taylor-Michaelson, and this is my mother."

Mom stood up from the desk, blushing a little. "You must be the Cobbs." She held out her hand. "I hope you had a good trip from Boston."

Travis, who had just come out of the kitchen anyway, poked Nikki at "from Boston."

"Yes, indeed," said Mr. Cobb. "Not much traffic in the city when we left yesterday."

"We got up at three in the morning," the small boy said proudly. "Dad had to do some business on the way, very early. He had to see..."

"This is Herbert Jr.," Mrs. Cobb interrupted. "He's hoping there'll be someone his age here to play with while Herb and I are house hunting." She smiled hopefully at Nikki and then at Travis.

Nikki studied Herbert Jr. dubiously; he looked about seven. "I'm twelve," she said, "and my brother's eleven."

"That's okay," the boy said. "I'm gifted."

"I'm sure Nikki and Travis would be happy to show your son around the place," Mom said. "Would you sign our guest book? Let's see, that was going to be MasterCard, wasn't it? Nikki, maybe you could get Louise to show the Cobbs their room. Travis, why don't you help with the suitcases?"

"Right you are, little lady," Herbert Sr. said heartily to Mom, producing a credit card. "Here you are. I'll take that big one, son," he said to Travis.

Nikki, pretending not to notice how Mom cringed at being called "little lady," went to the window into the kitchen, opened its partly closed shutters, and beckoned to Louise, who came out, introduced herself to the Cobbs, and led them upstairs.

"Are we going to have to play with that kid?" Travis whispered loudly to Nikki when she went to where he stood at the foot of the stairs with another of the Cobbs' suitcases. "I refuse. That's not in my job description."

"Oh, yeah? You ask Mom. I think it just got added. Maybe he won't be too bad."

But he was, at least most of the time. "This place is really falling apart," Herbert Jr. said later, looking disdainfully at the somewhat sagging front steps as Nikki and Travis led him outside. "We're going to look for a new house, probably with a lot of glass to let the light in. Mother likes plants."

"Mother?" Travis said nastily.

"That's my mother," Herbert Jr. said just as nastily. "I suppose you call yours Mom."

"How did you guess?" said Nikki. "I hope you'll find a house okay," she added. "Most of the ones we've seen around here are old."

"Not much glass." Travis picked up a rock and lobbed it into the woods. "Want to have a throwing contest?"

"No," said Herbert. "That's rather juvenile, don't you think?"

"What grade are you in anyway?" Nikki asked.

"Oh, I go to an ungraded school. I'm doing calculus now. I'm a math genius. Do you have a computer? I think I saw one when we came in."

"It's the inn's," Nikki told him. "It's only for inn business."

"That's all right," said Herbert. "I've got my laptop with me. I'm going to have to check my e-mail pretty soon."

"Why not now?" said Travis. "Now's as good a time as any."

"No, I think I'd like to finish the tour first. I always like to see my surroundings. What is THAT?" he demanded, pointing at the candlestone as they walked around to the back of the inn.

"That's what gave the inn its name," Nikki explained. "Everyone calls it the candlestone, and no one knows what it is. Or was."

"An ancient monolith, I should think."

Herbert Jr. walked excitedly around the stone. "Wonderful!" he said with surprising enthusiasm, peering more closely at the stone. "Look, there's carving on it." He pointed to a series of shallow lines and notches chiseled faintly along the stone's edges. "It looks like ogham. How marvelous!"

Nikki peered more closely at the carvings. She hadn't noticed them when they'd first seen the stone. "Ogham?" she asked.

"Yes, it's ancient Celtic writing. Usually Irish. The fact you've got this here could mean that this area was settled by ancient Celts. There's a theory that they came to New England thousands of years before anyone else. How exciting!"

Nikki examined the candlestone with new interest. Maybe Herbert wasn't so bad after all. She could see that Travis was thinking the same thing, but then he tugged at her arm and pointed to the driveway. A small blue Volkswagen beetle convertible was driving up.

"Whoops," she said to Herbert. "We've got to go. There's someone coming."

"You really do work here?" asked Herbert.

"Yes," said Travis. "We really do."

"That must be fun," Herbert said wistfully. "I wish I had a real job."

"You could," said Nikki. "Figure out what the writing on the candlestone says."

Herbert brightened. "Okay. I'll try. I'll copy it down first" — he whipped a notebook out of his pocket — "and then I'll get my laptop. I've got a program on ancient writing."

"Great." Nikki followed Travis around to the front of the inn in time to see a small gray-haired woman getting out of the Volkswagen. She was wearing a long blue skirt and a straw hat. As they approached, she took a cat carrier out of the car and Nikki's heart sank; they'd decided they had to have a no-pets policy at least for the first year, because of Max and Snowball and all the antiques. "Just till we see how it goes," Mom had said when Nikki had protested.

"Hello," said Nikki, trying not to look at the cat carrier. "Welcome to Candlestone Inn."

"Why, hello." The woman's sharp, birdlike nose didn't seem to match her wonderfully clear and sparkling blue eyes. She gave Nikki's hand a surprisingly vigorous shake. "I'm Hattie Fletch. And you are...?"

Nikki introduced herself and Travis. She was just trying to decide whether to say anything about the cat or leave that to Mom and Louise, when Hattie Fletch glanced down at the carrying case as if she'd read Nikki's mind and said, "Oh, it's not a cat. I'm an amateur geologist, and I find this is a good way to carry small rocks. I don't have any in here yet, so it's very light, but I hope to tramp around your beautiful countryside and see what I can find. It's so nice to be outdoors for a change instead of inside that stuffy museum!"

"Museum?" Nikki said quickly, and Travis raised his eyebrows as he reached for the suitcase that Miss Fletch now took out of the car.

"Yes, I'm head Egyptologist at a museum in western Massachusetts. And that means that I spend most of my time indoors with mummies and scarabs and models of pyramids." Miss Fletch threw her arms up in the air and took a deep breath. "It's wonderful to be outdoors, just wonderful. I can't wait to change into my rock-hunting clothes and get out on the trails. I've picked up some good maps, but maybe you could... why, hello, puppy!"

Max had bounded out the door, which Mom had just opened, and was greeting Miss Fletch like a long-lost friend.

"Scarabs," Travis whispered excitedly as Mom led Miss Fletch into the inn. "Did you hear her say *scarabs*?"

CHAPTER 7
A Clue in the Woods

"I sure did hear her say scarabs," Nikki replied. "And that," she added decisively, "makes her a suspect even if she's not from Boston. Maybe even Suspect Number One! Come on!"

She led Travis to her room, where she whipped her notebook off her desk and added:

SUSPECTS

1. Miss Fletch, because she's an Egyptologist, works in a museum, and mentioned scarabs

2. The hiker (the man who doesn't know who he is), because he had the scarab in his pack

Travis looked over her shoulder. "I'd make the hiker Number One," he said. "He *is* the one who had the scarab in his pack."

"I know, but..." Nikki thought a minute. "What if Miss Fletch put it there? I mean, the hiker said he didn't know anything about it. What if she planted it, as the sheriff said someone might have, without the hiker's knowing it, to throw suspicion off herself? And then what if she came here, figuring no one suspected her or had followed her, and was planning to get it back and sell it?"

"That might work. But did she hit him on the head, too? She doesn't look strong enough. Anyway, shouldn't we go see the hiker and ask him if he's ever seen her before or something?"

"Just what I was thinking," Nikki said. "Let's see if Mom or Louise knows where the hospital is and how to get there."

"We could unpack our bikes," Travis said eagerly, "at last."

But when Nikki and Travis went outside to get their bikes, which they'd decided to do before asking about the hospital, they found a very handsome youngish man with thick black hair and even thicker glasses standing in the driveway next to a green Honda and looking out over the lawn toward the pond. His tan corduroy suit was rumpled, especially the jacket, which looked a little damp, and the blue shirt he wore under it didn't look much better or much drier.

Nikki walked up to him while Travis was still staring. "Hi," she said. "I'm Nikki Taylor-Michaelson, and that's Travis. Welcome to Candlestone Inn. Or are you lost?"

"Hmm?" The man turned to face her, blinking as if he needed to focus his eyes despite the thick glasses. "Oh, no. No, I'm not lost. I'm checking in, actually." He held out a none-too-clean hand. "Name's Peter Jordan. Nice view you've got here. Sure beats the one out my office window!"

"Yes, it is nice," Nikki said primly. Then with an innocent look, she added, "Where's your office?"

"Downtown Boston," Mr. Jordan replied. "All I can see is the building next door."

"That's too bad," Nikki said with a significant glance at Travis. "Well, come on in and meet our moms. And register."

Peter Jordan appeared startled. "Moms? Oh, then you two aren't related. I see."

"We *are* related," Nikki said, and gave Mr. Jordan the same explanation she'd given a hundred times before, when pressed. "We're brother and sister, and both our moms adopted us when we were babies. They're life partners. Come on in."

"Life partners," Mr. Jordan said. "Oh. I see."

Nikki could tell that he didn't, but Travis quickly jumped in, saying, "Got any luggage?" and the man opened his trunk, taking out a large suitcase and a smaller blue one.

Within a very few minutes, he'd registered and gone up to his room.

"It's in town," Louise said a little later on her way outside in her gardening clothes with a pile of seed packets when Nikki asked how to find the hospital. "You go down our road in the opposite direction from the way to Don and Charley's..."

"And when the road forks," Mom said, looking up from a recipe book, open to COUNTRY MUFFINS, "you bear right and before you know it, you're there. I think I remember seeing the hospital on the left, but someone'll know." She glanced at Louise. "Do you really think they ought to bother that poor young man, though?"

"I don't see that it'll hurt," Louise answered. She had just picked up a looseleaf notebook and a basket containing an odd assortment of gardening supplies: plastic row labels, string, a trowel, a roll of aluminum foil, a black permanent marker, a cardboard can of something called "Sure Fire Legume Aide," and several items Nikki couldn't identify. "He did seem harmless. And if he still doesn't know who he is, we're his only friends. It might cheer him up, seeing the children."

"I suppose," Mom said. "If he's allowed to have visitors. He is — er — a suspect, after all."

Nikki and Travis edged toward the back door.

"The kids'll be safe in the hospital, Mindy," Nikki heard Louise say softly as they left. "Plenty of people around. Bikes are in the shed," she called after them. "I think. If not, try the barn."

"And watch where you're going along the road!" Mom added.

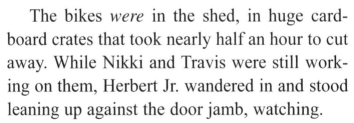

The bikes *were* in the shed, in huge cardboard crates that took nearly half an hour to cut away. While Nikki and Travis were still working on them, Herbert Jr. wandered in and stood leaning up against the door jamb, watching.

"At least he could offer to help," Travis muttered between clenched teeth, ripping savagely at a particularly reluctant piece of cardboard.

"Are those your bikes?" Herbert asked.

Nikki swallowed an impulse to say, "No, they're the President's." Instead she said, "Yes," and ripped at the cardboard savagely herself.

"Neat." Herbert came closer. "You don't have a third one, do you?"

"No." Travis inspected his brake cable. "We don't."

"The ogham's fake," Herbert said unpleasantly. "I thought you'd want to know. Someone must've wanted people to believe that the stone was ancient. But I bet it isn't. The symbols look like real ogham, but put together they don't make any sense."

Nikki tested her seat to make sure it was still firm and the right height. "Thanks for checking, anyway."

"Can I come with you?" Herbert asked. "Where are you going?"

"We've got something important to do," Nikki told him, trying not to sound quite as exasperated as she felt. "And there are only two bikes."

"I could rent one, maybe."

"You don't see a..." Travis began, but Nikki cut him off.

"Maybe you could later," she said kindly. "We'll look around and see if we can find a bike shop. That's something the inn should know about anyway," she told Travis when he rolled his eyes. "We should find some pamphlets about stuff like that and put them in the hall."

Travis pushed his bike out of the shed. "That's not what we're going for, though," he shouted as he shoved off and threw his leg over the bar, hopping onto the seat.

Nikki ran out behind him, swung onto her bike, and followed him down the driveway. "No, but it wouldn't hurt to look for some anyway. What a little worm," she said, glancing over her shoulder at Herbert Jr., who was standing forlornly back at the shed door. "At least he is sometimes."

"Most of the time," said Travis. "I sure hope he isn't staying long."

The inn driveway sloped gently down to the road, first between wide lawns and then between grassy meadows that were wider still, and punctuated with daisies. As she flew along, ahead of Travis now, Nikki looked up at the mountains. They showed blue through a light, high mist. Mysterious, she thought; I wonder if we'll ever climb them. I wonder if that poor hiker did; maybe he'll remember that much.

Then she reached the road, and the mountains were no longer visible. Thick woods rose on each side of her as she turned right and, dodging occasional puddled potholes, pedaled forward at a leisurely pace, enjoying the morning and the freedom of being outside.

Travis came up beside her, puffing a little.

"You're in the wrong gear," Nikki said pleasantly, "if you're out of breath. Either that or you've got pneumonia."

"Very funny." Travis shifted. "I did it on purpose. The wrong gear. I'm working on my leg muscles."

Nikki eyed him with amusement. Every few months, Travis went on a self-improvement kick of some sort, saying that inventors needed to be well-rounded. Last year it was eye-hand coordination, at least that was his explanation for spending what Louise called "an inordinate amount of time" playing video games. The year before that, it was memory. He'd gotten so he could rattle off every state capital, which a lot of the kids in his class could do, but Travis knew the states' populations and major industries as well.

"How come inventors need strong legs?" Nikki asked. "So they can run away from their customers when their inventions don't work?"

Travis speeded up, sticking his tongue out at her as he passed — and then he stopped suddenly, leaping off his bike. "Nik," he said in an odd voice, "look at this."

Nikki braked when she reached him, jumped off, and stared down at the dull red stains to which he was pointing. A succession of them marched in little drops across the road from the woods on one side to the woods on the other.

"A wounded animal," Nikki said, her veterinarian's instincts alert, "crossing the road. We'd better try to find it. It must have been hurt a while back, though. The blood's soaked in enough not to have washed away in the rain."

"Maybe it happened after the rain," Travis suggested quietly.

"I don't think so. It doesn't look fresh. And like I said, it's soaked in. Still, we'd better try to find whatever it is."

"How can we tell which way it went, though?"

"You take one side and I'll take the other," Nikki said. "Meet back here in ten minutes. That means go five minutes into the woods, and five back, even if you don't see any bloodstains. It won't do for us to go too far and get lost."

"There's a path," Travis observed, "on each side."

"So there is. Good. Five minutes your way and five minutes mine. Then back. Yell if you find anything."

Nikki plunged into the woods on the inn side of the road. The trees were mostly pines and the path was heavily carpeted with needles. There were a few dark spots where the needles seemed clumped together, maybe with blood, Nikki decided. Poor beast, she thought as she moved along. It must have been pretty big. A dog maybe; oh, I hope it's not a dog! Mentally, she reviewed what she'd learned about dog first aid last summer when she'd assisted Max and Snowball's vet. Keep a wounded animal warm; apply pressure to bleeding wounds...

"Nikki!"

Travis's voice sounded far away, but it was unmistakable.

Nikki turned. "I hear you!" she shouted. "What?"

"Come here! I think I've found something!"

Her heart racing, Nikki turned and ran back down the path, across the road, and along the path's continuation till she came to a small clearing among the pines. Travis was studying a patch of beaten-down grass near a single oddly twisted pine.

"Look." He pointed to a scrap of bright blue material caught on one of the pine's branches. Near it was a large dark stain on a rock.

"Whoa!" Nikki said softly. "So it wasn't an animal after all."

"It could have been. Maybe an animal bit someone who was wearing a blue shirt or a dress or something."

"Maybe," Nikki said dubiously, looking around. "Or fought with someone wearing a blue shirt or a blue dress. Or a person fought with another person. Look how the grass is flattened." She examined the rock, and then picked the blue cloth off the branch and put it in her pocket.

"The man who doesn't know who he is wasn't wearing blue," Travis pointed out. "In case you were thinking about him."

"I'm not sure what I was thinking," Nikki admitted. "Still, it could be important."

"Yeah, right," Travis said sarcastically.

Nikki ignored him and walked a few yards further along the path. "There's a sort of a brook," she said. "But no more blood. So that means that whatever happened, happened here. And then the — the victim, human or animal, but probably human — ran down to the road, crossed it, and went along the path I was on. So let's go back there."

"Nikki," said Travis when they reached the road. "Where are our bikes?"

CHAPTER 8
NEWS FROM BOSTON

Both of them stared in disbelief at the side of the road. "There was no one around," Nikki said. "No one."

"Someone obviously came along," said Travis.

"Or two someones." Nikki sniffed. "I think I smell car exhaust. So someone came along in a car..."

"...or a truck..."

"And swiped the bikes."

"But why?"

"Because," Nikki said angrily, "we were

dumb enough to leave them here. They're good bikes, after all. I can't believe we were so stupid! It's not as if we'd have done that back in the city."

"Yeah, but this isn't the city. I thought things were supposed to be safe in the country."

"Well, I guess they're not," Nikki snapped. "So far, we've heard that there's probably an art thief wandering around, and we've met a guy who was hit so badly on the head that he can't remember who he is, and someone put a horrible message on our car, and we've been following a bloody path in the woods, and our bikes have been stolen. That doesn't sound very safe to me."

"Nikki," said Travis, in an uncharacteristically shaky voice, "what are we going to do?"

Nikki pulled herself together. "I guess we'd better go on into town and see that guy. There'll be a phone someplace; we can call Mom and Louise and tell them about the bikes, and they'll come get us."

"Maybe we should tell the sheriff, too, or the cops, or someone. About the bikes, I mean."

"Right. Come on, let's go." Nikki set off at a brisk pace with Travis trailing sadly behind. She was more angry than sad, though. It's my fault, she thought bitterly. I should've known better. Dumb, dumb, dumb!

"Here's the fork," Travis said after about fifteen minutes.

"And there's the hospital, I bet," Nikki said when they'd turned and she'd spotted a wide brick building on their left. BENNET MEMORIAL HOSPITAL, said a neat black and gold sign on the front lawn.

"Where do we go?" Travis whispered when they got inside.

"First we find a phone and call Mom and Louise. Then we ask what room he's in...oh."

"Right." said Travis. "How can we ask what room he's in when we don't know who he is?"

"I guess we ask for the guy who has amnesia. Let's phone first, though. Do you have any money?"

Travis pulled an assortment of change and a couple of crumpled bills from his pocket.

"I owe you half." Nikki took a quarter and a nickel from him.

"It says thirty-five cents."

"I still owe you half," said Nikki, taking another nickel.

Louise answered after five rings, and when Nikki apologetically told her how dumb she thought they'd been to leave their bikes unattended, Louise just said, "You'd never have done it in the city; I'd probably have thought they'd be safe here, too." She said she'd pick them up in half an hour to give them time to visit the amnesia victim. "And then we'd better tell the sheriff about the bikes," she added.

"One down and one to go," said Nikki, after relaying all that to Travis. "Now for the hiker."

Travis in tow, she marched up to a semicircular desk in the hospital lobby. "Excuse me," she said to the middle-aged woman in pink sitting there. "We're looking for a friend of ours."

"Not quite a friend, really," Travis put in. "We don't know him very well..."

"We're from the Candlestone Inn," Nikki explained, and she went on to give the woman a shortened account of how they'd met the hiker.

Partway through, the woman interrupted. "Oh, you must mean our John Doe. That's the name they've given him. He's in Room 212. Second floor. Elevator's to your left." She sighed and clucked her tongue. "Poor boy. It must be dreadful to have amnesia."

"Yes, it must be," Nikki said politely. "Thank you."

John Doe didn't seem like a "poor boy" at all when they found him. He had a windowside bed in a four-bed ward with no one else in it, and they found him sitting in an armchair beside the bed, watching a Red Sox game on television.

"Well, hi," he said cheerfully when they approached. "It's the kids from the inn, isn't it? Nikki and — er —"

"Travis," Travis said. "Yes."

"How are you?" asked Nikki. "Any — any — you know?"

"Progress about who I am? No. I know I like baseball, though." He nodded toward the TV. "Lots of little things like that keep coming back. It's kind of weird. Like when they brought my breakfast this morning and there was coffee on the tray, I knew right away that I don't like coffee. Suddenly I knew I wanted tea instead. Isn't that weird?"

"Yeah," Nikki agreed, "but it must be reassuring, too. I mean, maybe bit by bit it'll all come back to you, you know?"

"Maybe."

"We have a question," Travis began, but Nikki cut him off.

"How's your head?" she asked.

"It still hurts. I've got one heck of a headache. They X-rayed me, though, and said nothing's broken." He chuckled. "Said I've got a hard head. Luckily, as it turns out. Those were pretty hard blows."

"What with?" Nikki asked curiously.

"They don't know. The usual 'blunt instrument,' they said."

"Do you remember anything more about it?" Travis asked.

John Doe shook his head. "Nothing. Nothing at all. Sometimes I think I'm just on the edge of it, of remembering, but then it slips away."

"When you're on the edge," Nikki asked, "do you ever remember a smallish woman with gray hair?"

"Or an old blue Volkswagen beetle?"

"No. Why?"

"There's a woman like that at the inn," Nikki explained. "She's an Egyptologist..."

"... and she mentioned scarabs."

"Not again!" John Doe exclaimed. "Someone else asked me about a scarab. Or the scarab. I really don't know how the silly thing got in my pack. Honest!"

Nikki tried to sit on the edge of the bed. It was too high, though, so she just leaned against it. "Who asked you? The sheriff, maybe?"

"Might have been, but I don't think so. It was last night — no, very early this morning. I was still pretty groggy. I don't even remember what he asked, exactly. He? Maybe it was a woman. It could have been a nurse, I guess, but I don't think so. Sorry."

"It's okay," Nikki told him. "You never saw one or had one or anything? A scarab, I mean?"

"I barely even know what one is. My grandmother had what she called a scarab bracelet. Wait!" he exclaimed. "My grandmother! I had a grandmother!"

"Yes?" Nikki prompted eagerly. "What about her?"

John Doe paused as if thinking, but after a few minutes, shook his head. "No," he said sadly. "No. I don't remember any more. Darn it!"

"Anyway," Travis suggested after a minute, "she had a scarab, right?"

"A scarab bracelet. Little sort of elliptical stones, different colors. She wore it all the time, I think."

"That's not the same kind of scarab." Patiently, Nikki explained again about the museum theft, in case John Doe's brain had been too fuzzy when he'd first woken up to take it all in.

"No," John Doe said. "I don't know anything about that. I'm sure I never saw that scarab till you showed it to me."

"It's at the museum in Boston now, being examined," said Travis. "And if it's the missing one, then..."

John Doe groaned. "Then I'm a suspect. So that's why they told me this morning the sheriff wants to see me later."

"Probably," Nikki said. "I think they might want to give you a lie detector test."

"I guess I can't lie if I don't have any idea what's going on or who I am or anything." He seemed almost cheerful again.

"Except for your grandmother," Nikki reminded him. "Maybe you should try to remember more about her." She looked at her watch. "I guess we'd better be going. Good luck with the sheriff. We'll probably come see you again, okay?"

"Okay. Sure. Thanks for coming this time and for filling me in. If one's going to be accused of a crime, it helps to know what the crime is!"

"He's pretty happy for someone who's got amnesia and who everyone thinks stole something worth half a million dollars," Nikki observed as she and Travis went down on the elevator.

"Maybe that's because he's sure he didn't do it. Or because he did do it, but he's got the perfect way to pretend he didn't as long as no one figures out the truth."

"Yeah, I know. He seems so calm now! I'd be really upset if I couldn't remember who I was or what I'd done and everyone thought I'd done something bad," she added as they got out of the elevator and headed across the lobby. "And I wouldn't be sure of anything. I like him, but I still think he's a suspect. Anyway," she said as they approached the door, "there's Louise."

The sheriff's office was next to the police station. "Why both?" Nikki asked as they went up the steps of the small white clapboard building.

"The police are just for local things," said Louise, who was wearing her clean jeans and shirt again, "and the sheriff's for county-wide things. I guess he has an office in each town he covers, for when he's there."

"Maybe it's the police we should tell about the bikes," said Travis, "if they're for local things."

"Maybe we should tell both." Louise knocked on the door marked SHERIFF.

"Come in!" boomed the sheriff's voice. "Oh, good," he said as they entered. "I was just about to call you folks. What can I do for you?"

Nikki explained about the bikes, and the sheriff, frowning, wrote down what she said. She also mentioned the bloody trail and rock, trying not to notice that Louise acted increasingly worried when Nikki mentioned more details than she had on the phone. The sheriff looked grave, too, as he wrote them down.

"I think," he said when Nikki had finished, "that you kids had better stay out of this from now on. It's beginning to look a little more serious than it seemed at first." He leaned his chair back in just the way Mom always said not to. "The museum in Boston called this morning," he told them. "That scarab you kids found isn't the real one. It's a very skillfully made imitation."

CHAPTER 9
SEARCHING

"We've got to search luggage, then," Nikki said to Travis when they got home and she'd hurried him upstairs to her room. The inn seemed to be bursting with people now. There was obviously no place downstairs for them to be alone, not even in the family quarters. Mom was bustling in and out getting things for people, checking them in, and answering the phone, too, which was ringing every few minutes. Louise took over that job as soon as she walked in with Nikki and Travis. Mom had advertised for a maid, and people were calling about that as well as about staying at the inn.

"Okay." Travis sat down on Nikki's bed. "But how come? I mean, if the scarab in John Doe's pack was a fake, that's sort of the end of the story, isn't it?"

"Maybe and maybe not." Nikki sat down at her desk, opposite him. "What if someone planted the fake scarab in John Doe's pack as the sheriff suggested before? You know, to make it look as if John Doe had the real one, and then the thief kept the real one?"

"Yeah, okay. But then why would the real thief be here? Or the real scarab?"

"They might not be. But they might be. Remember that map! And the thief would probably want to check on John Doe, if he planted the fake scarab on him — if John Doe's innocent. And he'd probably want to make sure people thought John Doe was the thief. He or she. Remember Miss Fletch."

"I'm with you there," Travis said. "Suspect Number One. Okay. Let's search her luggage."

Quietly, they unlocked the door to the public part of the inn; there was a key on the family side. Then they went down to the second floor and snuck along the hall to the white room, where Miss Fletch was staying. But just as they got to her door, Louise came around the corner with a vase of freshly cut lilacs. "What did we say about being in the guests' part of the inn?" she asked sternly.

"Oh — sorry," Travis said. "Right. We for-got."

"A likely story," Louise said mildly. "Anyway, Mom said to tell you it's time for lunch."

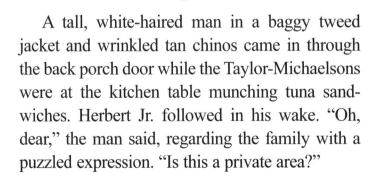

A tall, white-haired man in a baggy tweed jacket and wrinkled tan chinos came in through the back porch door while the Taylor-Michaelsons were at the kitchen table munching tuna sand-wiches. Herbert Jr. followed in his wake. "Oh, dear," the man said, regarding the family with a puzzled expression. "Is this a private area?"

"Yes." Mom stood up. "But that's okay, Professor. This is Professor Zorich from Harvard University," she said to the others.

"We've just been examining that wonderful stone." The professor beamed. "Young Herbert here thought the carvings on it were fake ogham, and you know, I think he's right in a way, but the symbols are pretty authentic. Do you have any literature about the stone?"

"No," Mom said. "I'm afraid not."

Louise put down her sandwich. "We wondered about it, too, when we bought the place. But we got distracted with renovations and learning how to be innkeepers and so forth. The real estate agent said it's a local mystery, and I'd love to find out more about it. But first we have to get the inn going."

"Hmm," said the professor. "I see. Maybe I can make some inquiries. Would you mind if I photographed the stone?"

"Not at all," said Louise.

Nikki moved her sandwich plate away from the edge of the table; Herbert had been eyeing it, and Max had been eyeing Herbert.

"Well, we'll be off," said the professor cheerfully. "Sorry to have burst in."

"You should have a sign on that porch saying private," Herbert Jr. shot over his shoulder as Mom opened the door to the dining room.

"I'll make one this afternoon," Travis promised. "Believe me."

"He's the ancient languages person, isn't he?" Louise asked when they'd gone and the Taylor-Michaelsons were alone again. "That professor? No wonder he's interested in the candlestone."

"That's right," Mom told her. "And I'm interested, too. But as you said, there hasn't been time to look into it. Lemonade?"

"Yes, please." Nikki held out her glass. "Isn't Harvard in Cambridge? Right near Boston?"

"Yes." Mom poured her some lemonade. "Why?"

"Oh, just curious," Nikki said with a glance at Travis, who nodded slightly. "Who else do we have? Guests, I mean."

"Just after you went upstairs," Louise said,

hastily swallowing a mouthful of tuna salad, "a Miss Dalrymple arrived." She chuckled.

Mom chuckled, too. "Honestly, it's not nice of me, but all I could think of was my mother calling an awful cousin of ours 'a long drink of water,' and that's exactly what this lady's like. I put her in the pink room. She's about — oh, how old would you say, Lou?"

"Anywhere from twenty-five to forty, I'd say. She's tall and very thin and pale, and her hair is sort of dirty blond and hangs in strings, and she holds her hands out in front of her, wrists bent, like a chipmunk when it stands up..."

"... and she has this tiny high-pitched voice," Mom put in, imitating it.

"...and she was terrified of Max."

"She did try to hide that."

"Aren't you setting us a bad example?" Travis asked, putting on what Nikki recognized as a mock shocked expression. "Saying awful things about people?"

"Yes, we are," Louise said. "You're right. But really, wait'll you see her."

There was a rap on the window to the main part of the inn.

"Speak of the devil," Mom whispered. "That's one of the guests, anyway." She got up and opened the shutter covering the window.

"I don't seem to have any towels," complained a strong male voice. Peter Jordan's face appeared in the window, scanning the kitchen myopically through his thick glasses and looking more than a little agitated.

"Oh, dear!" Mom sounded very flustered. "I'm so sorry. Nikki, would you just run up with Mr. Jordan to the linen closet and get him some towels? A big bath towel, a hand towel, and a face cloth, there's a dear. I gave him the deep blue room, to match his shirt."

Ordinarily, Nikki hated doing household errands, but the words "blue room to match his shirt" startled her, given the scrap of blue cloth they'd found on the pine branch. When she went through the kitchen door, she saw that Mr. Jordan's shirt was not only blue but was just about the same blue as that scrap and as rumpled as she remembered it — certainly rumpled enough to have seen some rough action. She remembered his shirt had looked damp earlier, too, although it didn't any more.

"Sorry about the towels," Nikki said, wondering how she could check the shirt for tears.

"Oh, that's all right." Mr. Jordan seemed relieved now that the problem was being taken care of. "Nikki, isn't it? Actually, I'm pretty sure I had towels this morning when I arrived, but I went out for a walk and when I got back just now they were gone. So I must not have had any, or maybe they were left over from the last guest and were removed by the maid."

"What maid?" Nikki almost said as she preceded Mr. Jordan up the stairs, but she stopped herself in time. It might not be good for business to admit they didn't have one yet. Instead she asked, "Where did you walk?"

"Along the road toward town." Mr. Jordan stopped outside his room while Nikki rummaged in the linen closet. "Pretty road."

"Yes. My brother and I went along it, too, on our bikes." She stopped suddenly; why hadn't they seen him, if he'd gone along the same road? Well, she decided, selecting towels, obviously he went at a different time.

Or he went a day or two earlier, and went into the woods, banged John Doe over the head, and...

"Here you are." Nikki turned, trying to see more of Mr. Jordan's shirt as she handed him the towels. Before she really had time, though, he was gone, and a wraithlike figure floated out of the pink room and down the stairs, giving her a wan smile as she passed. Miss Dalrymple, Nikki thought. She turned to go, but was stopped by a sudden high-pitched wailing from the lavender room, out of which burst a harassed-looking young woman with a baby bottle in her hand. She was wearing, Nikki noticed, brown shorts and a beige cotton shirt with an Egyptian-looking pattern on it — heads of pharaohs and Egyptian queens like pictures Nikki had seen during the Egyptian unit she'd had in school. "Oh," the woman said, stopping in front of Nikki. "Are you — I mean do you...?"

"Do I work here? Sort of. I'm Nikki Taylor-Michaelson and my moms run the inn." She pointed to the baby bottle. "Did you want to heat that up?"

"Oh, yes, please," the woman said gratefully. "If it wouldn't be too much trouble."

"No trouble at all." Nikki tried not to stare at the woman's shirt. "Here, I'll do it."

"Are you sure that you know... I mean, not everyone — and you're a bit young. I mean..."

Nikki laughed. "I've heated up plenty of bottles for baby animals. I worked at a vet's last summer. But come on down to the kitchen. My mom's heated baby bottles, and so has Louise, my other mom. We'll get it done. But you can do it yourself if you'd rather."

"Oh, yes, that's fine. I didn't mean..." The woman followed Nikki down the stairs, and her baby's wail floated thinly down after them.

While the bottle was heating, Mom introduced the woman as Mrs. Tansy, and explained that she and her husband and their baby — Abigail, three months old — had arrived while Louise was in town with Nikki and Travis. And after Mrs. Tansy had left, Mom said, "Right after the Tansys, the Woodwards came, a nice elderly couple. And that's the lot, thank goodness."

"We're full up!" Louise chortled. "Almost, anyway — six out of seven rooms full on our first day, Mindy." She and Mom exchanged a jubilant high five. "Business is booming."

"Yes," said Mom, "and I've told all of them about The Fox and Hare and I think most of them will end up there for dinner tonight."

"While we," said Louise, "have a quiet cook-out in the back yard. Steaks, to celebrate. I got some on my way to pick up the kids. I'll just change clothes again and see about cleaning up that old grill I saw in the barn before I finish planting the squash. Anyone who wants to give me a hand is welcome."

It took the better part of the afternoon to clean the grill, which had a lot of accumulated grease on it. But as Louise pointed out, at least the grease had kept the rust down. Herbert Jr.

wandered out while Nikki and Louise were working on it — Travis was making a PRIVATE sign — and Louise set him to scrubbing an extra narrow-mesh grill that she said could probably be used for things like fish that were likely to flake off and fall through the wide spaces on the regular grill. Nikki changed her mind about Herbert again, watching him work diligently. At least sometimes he wasn't too bad.

The guests did all leave at around dinner time, most of them to go to The Fox and Hare. Herbert Jr. seemed reluctant to go, and looked longingly toward the smoking grill, but his father grabbed him rather roughly by the arm and pulled him away.

After dinner, and after she and Travis had helped Mom and Louise clean up, Nikki took Travis aside and whispered, "NOW!" Mom was reading and Louise was working a crossword puzzle. Both of them were completely absorbed in what they were doing. Snowball was curled up on Mom's lap, and Max was snoozing on his cushion near the cold woodstove.

"We're just going out for a bit," Nikki said

when Mom looked up. "It's a nice night."

"Buggy, probably," Louise said absently, still absorbed in her puzzle. "Spray's on the shelf on the back porch."

"Thanks," said Nikki. "Stay, Max." And she and Travis went through the porch and outside, then around the side of the house to the front door.

"I feel like a thief," Travis whispered.

"Me, too. But we've got to do this. I don't think anyone suspects Miss Fletch, not even the sheriff. And now there's Mr. Jordan, too, maybe. And that professor's from Cambridge, although he seems unlikely. Fletch first, though. She seems most likely, except maybe she'd have more trouble than the others knocking John Doe out."

Quietly, they made their way upstairs and edged along the wall to the white room. They could hear Mrs. Tansy singing softly across the hall, to the baby, probably, but no one else seemed around.

Miss Fletch's cat carrier was under one of the white room's windows, full of rocks. Travis pointed to a small hammer lying on top of it.

"Blunt instrument," he said, picking it up and examining it. "But no blood."

"Still," Nikki said excitedly, "that could be the weapon." She turned to Miss Fletch's suitcase, an old-fashioned black one, which was on her bed, open.

"I bet it's not in the suitcase," said Travis. "If it were, she'd never leave it open."

"Maybe she's taken it out. Here, you look in the drawers and stuff, and I'll look in the suitcase. Quietly!" she added, when Travis jerked a drawer open with a bang.

"Sorry," he whispered. "It stuck."

"There's just — er — underwear in here. Lacy stuff." He giggled. "A nightgown, too. It's got..." He giggled again. "It's got green frogs on it."

Nikki couldn't help giggling as well when Travis held up a long flannel nightgown — nightshirt, really, white, with a pattern of bright green jumping frogs all over it.

"It's kind of cute, actually," she said.

Travis held it up to himself, mincing —

And just at that moment the door opened and Miss Fletch appeared on the threshold.

CHAPTER 10
ANOTHER PIECE
OF THE PUZZLE

ikki gasped.

"Would you like to try it on?" Miss Fletch asked dryly.

"No, I — er..." Travis was still holding the nightgown in front of himself, but gingerly now, as if it were hot. "I'm sorry, I..."

"When I was a girl," Miss Fletch said, taking the nightgown from him and putting it back in the drawer, "I had a teacher — fifth grade, I think it was — whose eyes were always red when she came to school in the morning. We used to joke about it. Old Red Eye, we called her, behind her back of course, and we used to pull our cheeks down to show the red part of our lower lids. Sometimes we did that when she was in class, if we didn't like what she said." Miss Fletch sat down in the armchair near the window. "One day," she went on, looking at Travis, "I stood up in front of the class before the first bell, pulling my cheeks down and pretending to be her. I'd just really gotten going and the class was dissolved in laughter, when the teacher walked in."

"Oh, wow," Nikki said softly. Travis just stared, but Nikki could see he was as embarrassed as she was.

"I ran to my seat, muttering 'I'm sorry,' but the next day we all went on mimicking her. I stopped, though, about a week later when I was visiting my grandmother in the hospital. I ran into the teacher in the hall. It turned out her husband was in the room opposite my grandmother's, slowly dying of cancer."

"So the red eyes," Nikki began, "were..."

Miss Fletch nodded. "Were because she spent every morning before school visiting him, and crying afterward."

"I'm really sorry," Travis said miserably. "Really, really sorry."

Miss Fletch's eyes sparkled again the way they had when she'd arrived. "I know you are. And I know that when one is young, one doesn't always think. Let's forget it, all right? But" — here she nodded toward the pile of clothes Nikki had flung onto her bed from the suitcase — "I'd really prefer that you'd tell me what you're looking for instead of going through my things." She waited expectantly.

"The scarab," Travis said before Nikki could stop him. Then he must have realized himself how foolish it was to mention it, for he clapped his hand over his mouth and stared wide-eyed at Nikki. "Oh," he squeaked lamely. "Whoops."

Miss Fletch smiled cryptically. "The turquoise blue jewel scarab stolen from the art museum down in Boston? News travels fast!"

Nikki was suddenly on her guard. What did Miss Fletch's smile mean? And why did she seem to know all about the scarab, maybe even more than they did? What about that hammer?

"The sheriff told us," Travis explained. "He thought... Ouch!"

Nikki had moved swiftly to his side and pinched his arm.

Miss Fletch was still smiling. "And you, being intelligent children, thought that because I work in a museum I might have some interest in the scarab. That's true." She stood up briskly. "I do. It's a very valuable artifact, and it would be terrible if it were lost to the art world and the viewing public." She put her hands out, shepherding Travis and Nikki to the door. "I'll keep my eyes open, of course. But I very much doubt the scarab's been brought here. This is a lovely inn and a lovely town, but I can't imagine why an art thief would hide out here, really, can you?"

"No." Quickly, Nikki shoved Travis out the door in front of her, hoping he wouldn't mention the map with the route to Bennet marked on it. "No. It was just a thought." She gave Miss Fletch her best fake smile. "We just thought it would be exciting. You know, pretending it might be here."

"Mmm," said Miss Fletch, and Nikki got the distinct feeling she hadn't been fooled for an instant. "And yet the sheriff..." Miss Fletch eyed Nikki closely. "No matter. See you later." She closed the door to her room, and Nikki heard the click of its lock.

"Suspect Number One," she whispered to Travis as they went back to the family wing. "Again. Never mind anyone else, at least for now. We'd better keep an eye on her. I wish we could see if there's a tear in that blue skirt of hers!"

But for the next two days, while Nikki and Travis were stuck with Herbert Jr., whose parents were off house hunting, Miss Fletch was out of the inn more than she was in it. She locked her door each morning when she left with her cat carrier, a box lunch Mom fixed for her — and her hammer. "It's for breaking rocks apart," she told Nikki when Nikki asked. And she came back each evening, dusty and tired, bent under the weight of the cat carrier. The second night, she left the cat carrier outside for a few minutes when she rushed in to take a phone call, and Nikki, on her way out with the trash, was able to peek inside it. But it was full of rocks again, uninteresting-looking ones at that.

The trash bin was more interesting, though, for Nikki spotted a heap of what appeared to be dirty rags at the bottom of it when she removed its lid to empty a wastebasket into it. But the heap wasn't dirty rags, she realized when she poked at it and then lifted it out. It was Candlestone Inn towels — bath towel, hand towel, and face cloth.

"Filthy," she said to Travis later, after she'd taken the sodden pile in to Mom and Louise, who said the towels must be the ones missing from Mr. Jordan's room, just as Nikki had guessed. "Absolutely filthy. Covered with mud and maybe also shoe polish. And soaking wet, too. So we'd better keep an eye on Mr. Jordan after all."

"Yeah, but why?" Travis asked. "Having a blue shirt and a bunch of dirty wet towels doesn't seem to have much to do with the scarab."

"Suppose," said Nikki slowly, "he was out in the rain with the scarab, and he saw John Doe and banged him over the head and put the scarab in his pack and came here and used the towels to dry himself off with?"

"He wasn't wet when he got here, though. And he wasn't dirty, just his hands, but only a little. You said the towels were filthy."

"His shirt was damp," Nikki said stubbornly. "And his jacket." But she had to admit Travis was right; Mr. Jordan hadn't been wet enough to have done all that — unless... "Unless he went someplace and, I don't know, dried his clothes off somehow, and then came here and used the towels to dry his face and stuff."

"Read my lips," Travis said. "THE TOWELS WERE SOAKING WET. ALSO FILTHY."

"Yeah, you're right," Nikki admitted. "Okay, so maybe that's not how it happened. But I still think the towels are one more piece of the puzzle."

"But which piece? As a matter of fact, which puzzle? The scarab? John Doe? Both?"

"I wish I knew," Nikki told him.

For the next couple of days, Nikki and Travis had to spend so much time entertaining Herbert Jr. that they were relieved when Mrs. Tansy asked if they could babysit while she and Mr. Tansy visited some friends. "It's her naptime," Mrs. Tansy explained, looking fondly down at the sleeping baby after Mom and Louise had agreed and Nikki and Travis reported to the Tansys' room. "She shouldn't be any trouble. This is so nice of you," she added, settling a large picture hat on her somewhat flyaway hair. "It's my old college roommate and her husband. We all went to school in Boston, and we haven't seen them in ages, since they moved up here. That's the main reason we came, you know, to see them..."

"Irma, let's go," interrupted Mr. Tansy impatiently.

"Yes, I'm coming. Her bottle's down in your kitchen," Mrs. Tansy said to Nikki. "Well, you know that. But she shouldn't need it. Still, if she cries you might try it. Or sing to her; she likes that. Clean diapers are — you do know about diapers, don't you?"

"Not a lot," Nikki admitted.

"But our moms do," said Travis, who had been standing awkwardly by the window.

"Yes, of course," Mrs. Tansy said. "When..."

"Irma!"

"Yes, coming, sorry."

And with an apologetic flutter of her hand, Mrs. Tansy finally followed her husband down the hall.

"Did you hear that?" Travis asked.

"Hear what?" Nikki was looking at Abigail. She really was rather cute, even though her face was sort of scrunched up.

"School in Boston." Travis moved to the dresser and started pawing through the pamphlets, belts, cosmetics, and other odds an'

ends on it. He picked up a small white box like the kind pins or earrings come in.

"Travis, no!" Nikki said as he opened it and held it up; it was empty except for a cushion of white cotton. "We can't search their room! Remember Miss Fletch. Besides, Mrs. Tansy must have been in college years ago. We don't even know if they live in Boston."

"It sounded like it."

"Yes, it did." Nikki sighed. "I wish we could search, too. But people would leave the inn in droves if they found out. We can't do that to Mom and Louise."

"No," said Travis after a minute during which he looked longingly at the two blue suitcases near the closet door. "We can't."

"Anyway," Nikki said, turning back to Abigail, who had squeaked in her sleep, "they don't seem much like suspect material anyway."

Abigail slept soundly until her parents came home two hours later, and Herbert Jr. was waiting for Nikki and Travis as soon as they emerged. So it was with great joy that they greeted the sheriff when he drove up and unloaded their bicycles later that afternoon.

"Where'd you find them?" Nikki asked, looking hers over quickly. But it seemed fine.

"Off in the woods. Just dumped there, probably."

"Where exactly?" Nikki asked.

"Oh, just off the road down from here, between here and town. I was on my way to see that boy in the hospital again — you know, John Doe — and take him his scarab, when a dog..."

"Wait," Nikki interrupted, making a mental note to ask about the dog later. "Take him his scarab? But..."

"The museum sent the fake one back," said the sheriff. "And I figured that since we'd found it in John Doe's pack, it might be his after all, legitimately, you know. And if so, I thought it might help him remember who he is. I wanted to tell him we've decided against the lie detector test, too, at least for the time being. So I was on my way to see him when a big short-haired dog ran across the road, sort of black and brown. She didn't seem to have a collar on, so I went after her, and there were your bikes."

"Thank you." Travis fondled his bike as if it were a long-lost friend.

"Don't mention it. I never did find the dog. She must be a stray. Skinny. And I'm not sure but what she'd been hit, you know, by a car. There was some blood on her."

"Could you show us where you saw her?" Nikki asked, her vet's instincts pulling her thoughts away from John Doe and the scarab, at least for the moment.

"You can't miss the spot." The sheriff climbed back into his car. "About a mile beyond your driveway, right by an electric pole. Utility Pole Eight. You'll see the number on the pole. Be careful, though, if you run into her. Strays aren't always friendly." He started the car. "My best to Mindy and Louise," he said, waving as he drove off.

"Nikki," Travis said urgently. "John Doe..."

"I know. I think we should see him again, too, in case he remembers anything more about the scarab now that he has it again. But if the dog's hurt... We'd better look for her on our way to see John Doe. Let's hurry, though, before Herbert Jr. asks to come."

Herbert Jr. was running around to the front of the inn with a butterfly net when Nikki and Travis hopped on their bikes and pedaled off. "Wait!" he called after them.

But neither of them heard.

This time they took their bikes with them when they went off the road, despite the fact that it was awkward pushing them through the woods. There was no sign of a dog near Pole Eight, though, so they decided to see John Doe quickly and then conduct a more thorough search on their way home from the hospital.

John Doe was sitting in his chair again, dressed in a rather tattered yellow shirt and jeans, watching another ball game. There was someone in one of the other beds this time, but he looked either asleep or unconscious.

"Seven to nothing," John Doe said as Nikki and Travis walked in. "We've got a real pitching problem this year." He aimed the remote at the set and clicked it off.

"Hi, John," Nikki said. "We..."

"Michael."

"Huh?"

"Michael. I think my name's Michael. I don't know about the last name, but Michael keeps popping into my head."

"Hey, that's great!" Travis exclaimed. "That must make you feel better."

"Some. But only some. It's frustrating, too."

"Anything else?" Nikki asked cautiously, perching on the long, low air-conditioning-heating unit. She could see the fake scarab sitting on the bedside table. "The sheriff said he gave you the scarab back. And that it's not the stolen one, but an imitation."

"Yes, he told me," Michael answered. "But it doesn't help. Except I'm sure I never saw it before I woke up in your inn. You want it? It seems to me you have more use for it than I do."

"No," said Travis grandly, "that's okay."

"Sure," Nikki said simultaneously, for an idea had just begun forming in her mind. "Yes, thanks. At least maybe we could borrow it. Could we?"

"Help yourself." Michael waved his hand toward the scarab.

So Nikki pocketed it, and after a few minutes' conversation about the Red Sox and the man in the next bed, who'd just had an operation, Nikki and Travis hurried out to look for the dog again.

CHAPTER 11
THE STRAY

They found the dog huddled not far from the rock where they'd found the blood and the tree that had held the fragment of blue cloth; an overgrown path led there through the woods, it turned out, from Pole Eight. She was indeed collarless and painfully thin. There was caked blood on her side.

"So," said Travis, "the blood we saw the other day must have been hers."

"Maybe. But maybe not. I don't think we can be sure. A lot of time's gone by." Nikki knelt ten feet or so from the dog. "Poor girl," she crooned softly, motioning Travis to stay back. She held out her hand. "Good girl. Good girl. It's okay. We won't hurt you. Good girl. You must be hungry. What a good girl." Still talking softly, Nikki edged closer to the dog, who she could see was trembling. But she wasn't running away either, or snarling.

Nikki stopped a couple of feet away from her.

"Why don't you just grab her?" Travis whispered.

"Because that'll frighten her," Nikki said in the same soft voice she'd been using for the dog. "Good girl. If she comes to me then she won't run away from us when we try to take her home. At least she might not. But if I grab her, she's sure to. Look."

The dog stretched her nose out and touched Nikki's hand.

"Good girl." Nikki held perfectly still. "Good, good girl. That's it."

The dog licked her. Slowly, Nikki moved her hand around to the top of the dog's head and scratched her ears gently.

The dog gave a sad little moan, and her skinny tail thumped on the grass. A moment later she was in Nikki's arms, licking her face and whimpering.

"It's okay, girl." Nikki snuggled her face against the dog's neck. "It's okay. We're going to take you home and fix you up."

"Is she hurt badly?" Travis asked, coming closer.

The dog stiffened.

"Careful, Trav. She doesn't seem to be very trusting. I'm not going to look at her wound till we get her home. Hold your hand out to her the way I did."

Travis held his hand out, and Nikki touched his shoulder to show the dog he could be trusted, too. In a few minutes the dog wagged her tail and licked Travis's hand. Then, when Nikki let go of her and, moving away, called softly, the dog trotted willingly beside her. "Thank goodness," Nikki said as they pushed their bikes back to the road. "I don't see how we'd have gotten her home if I'd had to carry her."

"You've got the scarab, right?" Travis asked when they'd been walking along the road for a while.

Nikki patted her pocket. "I've got the scarab. And I've got plans for it, too."

"Like what?"

"Like you'll see."

"Come on!"

"This scarab," Nikki said dramatically, patting her pocket again, "is going to be a trap. Only we all have to be part of the plan, and I'm still figuring it out."

"All who?"

"All Taylor-Michaelsons. Mom, Louise, you, me. Not the guests. The trap's for them. You'll see. But," she added, as they turned into the inn's driveway and began climbing the long slope up to the house, "first we have to take care of our new friend here." She reached down and patted the dog, who wagged her tail again, a little faster this time.

The stray dog wagged her tail once more when they had her settled in the kitchen on a heap of cushions and towels next to Max's bed by the wood stove. Max had touched noses with her right away, licked her face, and sniffed her all over, so that was all right. Snowball had retreated to the top of the refrigerator, from where she watched disdainfully while the Taylor-Michaelsons fussed over the dog.

"I wonder what her name is," Mom said, bending down with a small bowl of moistened kibble. "Only a little," Nikki had warned. "She's half starved and she'll be sick if she has a lot right away, even if she wants it."

"I wonder what happened to her." Louise ran her hand gently over the dog's shoulder and examined her flank. "What do you think of this, Nik? It looks like a bruise as much as a cut."

Nikki examined the wound. It did look like a bruise, sort of, although that was hard to see even though the dog's hair was short. The caked blood hid it, too, but there didn't seem to be a deep cut.

"It's like someone kicked her," said Travis.

"That's exactly what it's like." Mom peered down over the dog's head. The dog was gulping down the kibble as if she was afraid someone would take it away before she was finished.

"There, there, stray," crooned Louise, patting her. "It's okay. No one's going take your food away."

"Max would if he could." Travis pointed to Max, who was sitting nearby, drooling, his tongue lolling out and his eyes on the bowl of kibble.

Nikki gave him a dog biscuit.

"What do you think, Nikki?" Louise asked again. "Should we take her to the vet? Or do you think you can handle it?"

Nikki studied the wound again. "I think I can clean it up. And if nothing's broken..." Gently, she touched the dog's flank, pressing a little when the dog didn't seem to object. "Poor girl," she said softly as she probed. "Poor stray."

"Stray," said Travis. "Maybe that's what we should call her."

"It's not a very elegant name," Mom pointed out.

"But she's not a very elegant dog," said Louise. "She's a lovely dog, and a sweet dog, and a gentle dog. But not an elegant dog."

"Yeah," said Nikki, "but calling her Stray would be like calling someone Orphan. She's probably got a perfectly good name."

"Like Michael," said Travis. "But she can't tell us what it is any more than he could."

"Who's Michael?" asked Mom, so Travis, who seemed to like him better now that he knew his name, explained while Nikki washed the dog's wound.

"It does seem to be mostly a bruise," Nikki said when she'd finished. "And I guess we should take her to the vet. I mean, I don't think anything's broken, but I can't really tell without an X-ray. And the wound was kind of dirty. Maybe she should be having antibiotics."

"I agree." Louise straightened up. "I'll take them, Mindy."

"Okay," Mom said. "I'll call the vet."

In a moment she was back, saying the vet had said he could see them right away. Nikki found an old collar of Max's and snapped an extra leash onto it. They all took the dog out for a quick walk around the yard before putting her in Louise's car, and Nikki, Travis, and Louise had just climbed in themselves when Professor Zorich and Herbert Jr. came bursting out of the house, waving frantically.

CHAPTER 12
ONE MORE CLUE

"Now what?" Louise rolled down her window.

"Wait! Stop!" Herbert Jr. was shouting.

"We're standing still," Travis pointed out. "We haven't gone yet."

"What's the matter?" Mom asked, sounding alarmed.

"The — the telephone," Herbert said breathlessly, rushing to Louise's window. "On the telephone. Just now. A — a voice..."

Louise sighed. "Did we forget to put the machine on?"

"No, no." The professor had reached the car

by then, very red in the face. "I'm sure you didn't. It's just that Herbert and I were passing through the hall on our way out for a walk to the town library to look up more about ogham when it rang. Herbert, like the responsible lad he is, picked it up, and..."

"...and," said Herbert importantly, "it was a THREAT! A real threat."

Mom and Louise exchanged a worried glance, and Nikki and Travis exchanged an excited one.

"What do you mean?" Mom asked cautiously.

"What kind of threat?" asked Louise.

"Someone," said Herbert with obvious relish, "with a really deep voice, kind of fake-sounding, said, 'KEEP AN EYE ON YOUR CHILDREN.' "

Mom and Louise looked extremely alarmed. "Anything else?" Mom asked.

"Yes. I said, 'What?' because I wasn't sure I'd heard right, and the voice said the same thing again. 'KEEP AN EYE ON YOUR CHILDREN,' and then it said, softer, 'If you know what's good for you.' And then whoever it was hung up."

"Was it a man or a woman?" Nikki asked.

"A man."

"Sorry," the professor apologized. "I took the phone then and tried to engage the prankster in conversation, but..."

"...but he'd already hung up," Herbert said. "I was the only one who heard him," he added proudly.

"Bully for you," Travis muttered under his breath. He sounded a little envious, though, too, Nikki thought.

"Thank you, Herbert," Mom said.

"Maybe next time the phone rings," said Louise, "we'd better let the machine answer. That way if whoever it is calls again, we'll have a recording of the voice."

"Oh, very good," the professor said admiringly. "What a good idea!"

"If I were making threats on someone's phone," said Nikki, "I wouldn't do it on a machine. I wouldn't want my voice recorded."

"Good point." Louise started the car. "But it still won't hurt to try. Anyway, it probably was just a prank. Thank you, Herbert, and thank you, too, Professor Zorich."

"Any time," said the professor. "Come along, Herbert."

"A prank like the note on the car at the restaurant was a prank?" Mom said, leaning through the driver's side window when the professor and Herbert had left. "I don't know, Louise. It seems a little too coincidental to me."

"To me, too," Nikki said.

"Yeah," Travis agreed.

Mom turned toward both of them. "Prank or no prank, I want you both to stick around the inn from now on. No going off alone on your bikes. There've been too many unsettling things happening. Until we get to the bottom of this, you're to stay on the inn grounds. Right, Louise?"

"Absolutely. Got it, guys?"

"But..." Travis began.

"No buts," Mom looked stern and worried as Louise headed down the driveway.

The vet was a very young man. "Just out of vet school, I bet," Louise whispered when they took the dog into his examining room. "Maybe not a lot of experience."

"He'll know more," Nikki whispered back. "He'll know all the latest things."

"Well, well," the vet, whose name was Dr. Gismer, said enthusiastically, "what do we have here?" He beamed at Nikki and Travis.

"A dog," Travis said innocently.

Nikki giggled. "At least he didn't wink," she whispered to Travis.

Louise lifted the dog onto the examining table. "The children found her," she said, "in the woods. Nikki — that's our daughter — cleaned her wound up a bit, but my partner and I thought it would be a good idea for you to take a look."

"Yes." Dr. Gismer's face was very serious now. "Good girl," he said to the dog, patting her. "Good girl."

The dog licked his hand.

"He's okay," Nikki whispered to Louise. "Look how she likes him. He's not hurrying, either. Some vets do. It scares the animals."

"I should think so," Louise whispered back. "Scares me, too, when a doctor hurries. Unless I want to get whatever it is over with."

"It looks as if she's been kicked," Dr. Gismer said angrily. "Quite hard." He carefully cleaned her wound with antiseptic. "You did a good job," he said to Nikki. "I just want to make sure there won't be any infection."

Nikki nodded.

Dr. Gismer finished cleaning the wound. Then he looked in the dog's ears, her eyes, and her mouth. "Odd..." He took a pair of long tweezers from his supply cabinet and pulled something from between the dog's back teeth. "Here's a bit of blue cloth. Funny. She must've run into that while she was looking for food."

Nikki poked Travis.

"Whoa," Travis breathed.

"I'll just take her out back and X-ray her," Dr. Gismer went on. "To make sure her ribs are okay. You should probably keep her confined

145

for a couple of days till she's feeling better, especially if you have other animals. Or I could keep her here for you."

"No." Nikki turned to Louise. "Please?"

"Where?" asked Louise.

"There's the barn," Nikki reminded her.

"I could make her a pen," Travis offered.

"Okay," Louise agreed at last. "But we should advertise for her owner, just in case."

Nikki made a face, but she knew she couldn't argue against that. If it were Max, lost and hurt, she knew she'd want whoever found him to advertise, too.

The dog's ribs turned out to be fine, and soon the Taylor-Michaelsons were on their way home again with her and a bottle of antibiotic pills to be given twice a day for ten days, just in case. Nikki asked Dr. Gismer for the piece of blue cloth, and he dropped it into a plastic bag which she stowed in her pocket along with the fake scarab.

"Tonight," she whispered to Travis on the way home, "we'll set that trap."

CHAPTER 13
BLUE CLOTH

O n the way home they stopped off at the sheriff's office and left a note for him about the phone threat, and when they got home, the answering machine was blinking. "I decided to wait for you before I listened to it," Mom told them.

Nikki, still holding the leashed dog, whom she'd decided to call Lady, pushed the play button.

But it wasn't another threat.

"Hi, Taylor-Michaelsons," came a cheerful voice. "It's Michael here, you know, John Doe. The hospital says I'm okay now — no concussion — and they say they can't keep me any longer but they want me to check in every day at their outpatient department so they can try to help me figure out who I am. The thing is that I need a place to stay. I don't seem to have any money, but I wondered if I could do odd jobs for you at the inn for a while in exchange for a bed and maybe a little pocket money so I can get meals. There's a cheap diner in town. I really don't want to impose, though, so please say no if it won't work out. I'll wait to hear from you; I'm still at the hospital. Bye!"

"Yes," said Travis eagerly. "Let's let him stay. He's really pretty neat."

"He is nice." Nikki was also thinking that it would be a lot easier to keep an eye on him if he were staying at the inn.

"But where will we put him?" said Mom. "We're full up except for the light blue room, and we really should keep that open in case someone stops by."

"In the East Wing?" Travis suggested. "You said there were more rooms there."

"We also said the East Wing's not ready,"

Louise reminded him. "And not safe."

"He wouldn't mind roughing it," Nikki said, "I bet. He's a camper, after all."

"That may be," said Mom. "But — oh, look, I'd like to be friendly, but we don't know anything about him, and the sheriff did say to be careful. Besides, what odd jobs could he do?"

"We don't know much about our other guests either," Louise pointed out. "And we still do need a maid."

Mom laughed.

"Well, we do."

"Maybe Charley and Don need someone," Nikki suggested; she could see that Mom wasn't going to give in.

"Or maybe he could cut the grass here," Travis put in. "That would be a big help."

"A big help to you, you mean," Louise said. "That's your job, remember?"

Mom reached for the phone. "I like the idea of Charley and Don. They look as if they can take care of themselves. And with any luck, they'll have a guest room."

"But Mom..." Nikki began.

"Nikki, I know you like Michael and I know it would be exciting to have him here, but since we don't know anything about him, I think it would be a lot less risky if he weren't here. After all, we have gotten those threats. And Charley and Don should be able to take care of themselves and each other. They don't have two children and a lot of paying guests to protect the way we do."

"They've got people eating with them," Nikki said.

"Suppose he poisons them?" Travis grinned.

Louise made a face.

"All the more reason for his not staying here," Mom said firmly. "Besides, if he's not a poisoner, he can get meals as well as a room with Charley and Don. Here all he can get is a room."

"And muffins," said Travis. "You're forgetting the muffins."

"Man cannot live on muffins alone," said Louise. "Go ahead, Mindy, call."

Charley confirmed that he and Don did have a guest room and said they'd been looking for an extra person to help in the kitchen anyway.

They'd be glad, he said, to give Michael a try. They had some new kitchen equipment to pick up and install; they were closing the restaurant for the evening so they could work on it. Could Michael stay at the inn till late afternoon when they'd be on their way back with the equipment? They'd stop by then and collect him.

"I told him yes," Mom said after explaining all that. "He could eat supper with us, I suppose, if they're late."

"Spaghetti," Louise said promptly. "We've got tons of it. I'll just go start some sauce." She bustled off to the kitchen.

"Yum!" said Travis. Louise's spaghetti sauce, which was almost the only thing she ever cooked, was a special favorite of his; he even asked for it on his birthday every year.

"Goodness," said Mom, "I've got an applicant for the maid's job coming in twenty minutes. Come on, guys. Into the family quarters or outside."

"Here, Lady," Nikki said to the dog. "Time to get you settled. Travis, you come, too. Bring those cushions from the sitting room, would you?"

Mr. and Mrs. Cobb drove up just as Nikki and Travis were crossing the lawn with Lady; Travis was carrying a pile of cushions, and they'd left a disconsolate Max in the kitchen. "We shouldn't let Max play with her," Nikki had said, "till she's healed."

"Poor Max," Travis said, and then the Cobbs' car drove up.

"Why, hello, there!" Mrs. Cobb climbed out of the car in another flowered dress. "It's the inn children, isn't it? And their dog, too. Nice doggie." She held out her hand to Lady, who wagged her tail.

"Not our dog," said Nikki. "She's..." Nikki stopped then, for Travis had poked her, and was nodding toward Mr. Cobb, who, dressed in ordinary clothes this time, had just gotten out of the other side of the car and was coming around toward them...

...and stopping, just as Lady suddenly lifted her head and stiffened, staring straight at him. The hair on the back of her neck rose, and she growled.

"Lady, no!" Nikki shouted, jerking her leash the way one does when giving a dog a "correction" in obedience school.

But Lady went right on growling.

"Oh, dear," said Mrs. Cobb, "it must be that awful after-shave, Herbert. You know," she explained confidentially to Nikki and Travis, "it's a funny thing, but our own dog — Noodle, his name is — hates it, too." She lowered her voice as if sharing a secret. "Frankly, I don't like it much myself. But Herbert insists on using it, and we thought that here, anyway, with Noodle at the kennel, it would be all right..."

But Nikki wasn't paying any attention to Mrs. Cobb. She was watching Mr. Cobb instead, who'd stopped in his tracks, his eyes narrowing as they'd turned toward the dog. The odd thing was that he seemed more angry than afraid.

"Come, Lady," Nikki ordered, tugging at the leash. "Come on. Heel."

Lady gave one last growl — a real snarl, actually, with teeth bared — in Mr. Cobb's direction, and then obediently fell into step beside Nikki.

Travis, still carrying the cushions, was shaking when they got to the barn. He edged away from the dog. "That was awful. She'd have torn him to pieces."

"Yes," Nikki agreed, "but she wouldn't have torn Mrs. Cobb to pieces. It was as if she knew him, Travis. If she were vicious, she'd be weird with everyone, not just one person. Of course it might have been the after-shave, but I don't think so. It's like she knew him."

"Maybe she used to be his dog and he abused her. He looks like the kind of guy who might do that."

"Yes," Nikki agreed. "He does. But Mrs. Cobb didn't seem to know her, and she didn't seem to know Mrs. Cobb." Nikki took the cushions from Travis and laid them in a corner of the barn. "We could ask Herbert Jr. You know, ask casually about Noodle and the after-shave and his dad and dogs."

"Good idea. But Herbert went to the library with Professor Zorich, remember?"

"They have to come back sometime. Meanwhile, we'll need a water dish and a food dish for Lady. And it really would be cool if you'd build her that pen. Then we can use it for other strays, too, if we find any."

"Right. I think I saw some hardware cloth in the shed, and I know there's lots of scrap wood."

"What's hardware cloth?"

"It's like very heavy, very wide-mesh screening. I'll just go get it, and tools and some paper and a ruler and a pencil..."

"And a water dish and a food dish," Nikki called after him. Then she settled down on the cushions with Lady, who seemed content to lie there next to her, her head on Nikki's lap.

It was odd, Lady's reaction to Mr. Cobb. And Mr. Cobb's reaction to her. That should probably go in the notebook, she decided, along with the other new developments, even though it's hard to see any connection to the missing scarab. Maybe there are two separate sets of mysterious things going on, she thought: the missing scarab, the fake scarab, and Michael — and maybe the threats — as one set, and Lady and the bloody rock and the blue cloth and Mr. Cobb...

Blue cloth.

Nikki sat up straighter.

There was Miss Fletch's skirt, of course, and Mr. Jordan's shirt. But hadn't Mr. Cobb been wearing a bright blue shirt when he'd arrived at the inn the other day?

CHAPTER 14
BESS

It was no good trying to get into the Cobbs' room to look for the blue shirt, for Mr. and Mrs. Cobb had gone straight up the stairs to it, and had closed the door. While Louise worked in the front garden and Mom hung sheets out to dry and Travis stapled the hardware cloth to a frame he'd made of one-by-three boards he'd found in the shed, Nikki sat on the front steps with Lady. She'd gotten her notebook from her room and was copying her earlier entries over after bringing them up to date and adding to them:

STOLEN TURQUOISE SCARAB
1. Stolen from Boston art museum
2. Considered valuable

MYSTERIOUS HIKER
1. Lost; head wounds; amnesia
2. Turquoise scarab in pack
    a. Turned out to be fake
3. Doesn't remember what happened
    a. Remembered grandmother
    b. Remembered Red Sox (Boston team)
    c. Remembered name is Michael
4. Faking?

MAP
1. Found in museum near scarab's case
2. Route marked from Boston to Bennet

THREATS
1. Note on car: "Mind your own business"
2. Phone call: "Keep an eye on your children if you know what's good for you"
3. Connection to theft?

STOLEN BIKES
1. Stolen from road near path to bloody rock
2. Found near Pole 8

BLOODY ROCK
1. In woods at end of path from where bikes were stolen
2. Other path leading to rock from Pole 8
3. Blue cloth on pine branch near rock

HURT DOG
1. Found near bloody rock
2. Blue cloth in dog's teeth
3. Dog growled at Mr. Cobb

SUSPECTS
1. Miss Fletch
   a. Egyptologist
   b. Works in a museum (W. Massachusetts)
   c. Says she collects rocks, but knew about scarab

    d. Was wearing blue skirt

    e. Has hammer

2. Michael (hiker)

    a. Had fake scarab in day pack

        1) Note: Where's sleeping bag, etc.?

    b. Could be faking amnesia

3. Mr. Cobb

    a. Dog doesn't like him

        1) Dog's connection to scarab?

    b. Was wearing blue shirt

    c. From Boston

4. Mr. Jordan

    a. Blue shirt

    b. Missing towels/dirty towels

        1) Might not be his fault. Could someone else have taken them?

        2) Why?

    c. Works in Boston

Nikki sighed. It was discouraging. Even though there was a lot of information, very little of it seemed to fit together. Maybe we really are dealing with two separate incidents, she thought again. Michael and the dog and the cloth and the bloody rock. Or the dog and the bloody rock and the bikes and Mr. Jordan and Mr. Cobb. Or the missing scarab and Miss Fletch, and Michael.

What about the threats?

They seemed more serious than the other things, more like something a real criminal would do. So, she decided, they must have to do with the scarab.

But which scarab?

Maybe there's really no connection between the fake one and the real one.

No, she thought. That would be too much of a coincidence. There has to be a connection...

Suddenly, just as Travis came out of the barn calling, "Pen's ready," Lady pulled at the leash Nikki had looped casually over her knee. "Lady!" Nikki shouted, trying to grab the leash as the dog hurtled away from her. "Lady, no!"

Michael, looking cheerful and healthy, with his pack slung over one shoulder again, was coming up the driveway, waving as he came...

...And Lady, tail joyfully wagging, leash dragging, was running to meet him!

Louise stood up from the garden just as Lady threw herself at Michael, jumping on him, licking his face, wagging her tail so hard it looked in danger of coming off, and moaning.

Michael froze for a split second. Then, with a cry of "Bess! Oh, my God!" he dropped to his knees and took the big dog in his arms, hugging her and laughing and sobbing at the same time.

CHAPTER 15
THE MISSING LINK

For a minute or two everyone stood there quietly, smiling, watching Michael and the dog. Nikki was bursting with questions and she could see everyone else was, too, but it was obvious that no one wanted to interrupt the happy reunion.

In a while, though, Michael looked up, still kneeling with his arms around the dog, his eyes shining and tears glistening on his cheeks.

"I'm Michael Fogarty," he said quietly, with great certainty. "And this is my dog, Bess. I remember now. Oh, thank God, I remember!" He buried his face in Bess's short hair for a moment and then stood up. "Sit, Bess," he said softly, and Bess sat beside him, panting and looking up at him lovingly. "Good girl," said Michael. "Good girl."

"I think," Louise said briskly, "that this calls for a celebration. Let's all go inside and have some lemonade."

"Good idea," Mom agreed. "Come on, Michael Fogarty. Come on, Bess."

But Michael was looking at the wound in Bess's flank. "What's this, girl?" he said softly.

Nikki explained.

"That — that louse!" Michael said angrily, standing up. "I could kill him!"

"What louse?" Louise asked as they walked toward the house.

"You'd better begin at the beginning." Mom led everyone through the back door. "Lemonade first, though — Nikki, glasses, please. Travis, napkins and the cookie jar."

So for a few minutes the Taylor-Michaelsons bustled around setting things out, while Michael sat at the kitchen table with Bess's head on his knee. Max sniffed at Bess's other end and then crouched hopefully on his forelegs, clearly wanting to play, and Snowball watched from her usual lofty position on top of the refrigerator.

"Now," said Mom when the table was set and the lemonade poured, "let's hear all about it."

"Well," Michael began, "I'm Michael Fogarty, as I said, and I live in Boston." He shook his head. "Amazing. It's all come back in a rush, my whole life, who I am, everything."

"And who," Louise prompted gently, "are you besides being Michael Fogarty, Bess's owner, who lives in Boston?"

"Michael Fogarty, sculptor," Michael answered. "At least that's who I want to be, but of course commissions don't grow on trees and I'm not famous or anything. I work as an assistant museum curator so I can eat, and..."

"Where?" Nikki asked.

"At that big art museum in Boston," Michael told them. "It's a great place to work, for artists, anyway."

"What — er— section?" Nikki persisted intently.

"What do you mean?"

"What part of the museum?"

"No special part. We get moved around. I've worked in lots of sections."

"Egypt?"

"Yes, I've worked in the Egyptian section. Not too recently though, but...oh." Michael stopped abruptly, staring at her. "I see what you mean," he said slowly. "Oh, my."

Mom and Louise looked as if they were just beginning to catch on, and Travis was nodding.

"Anyway," said Nikki, "go on. About what happened, I mean."

"Okay." Michael continued. "I had a vacation coming to me, and although I usually spend vacations working — sculpting, I mean — or taking classes, I decided this time I needed to do something different. So I decided to come up here to Vermont and do some hiking. Old Bess" — he rubbed her ears fondly — "needed some exercise, too, so we set out."

"Did you tell people at the museum where you were going?" Travis asked.

"Sure, I guess so. I said I was going hiking, anyway."

Nikki moved closer to Michael. "Did you tell anyone in particular, though?"

"Nikki," Mom said gently, "let's let Michael tell the story his way."

"Yes, but Mindy," Louise put in, "I think the kids are on to something." She turned to Michael. "Do you remember how you got hurt?"

"Yes, I think so. Some of it, anyway. Early that morning I'd gone off the trail a bit to explore a smaller path, and I found an interesting pine tree in a clearing" — Nikki glanced at Travis — "and I thought it might be a shape I could use in a sculpture I'd been thinking about. So I wanted to look at it more closely. I heard some rustling in the woods alongside me and behind me, and Bess acted nervous, but I thought it was probably deer or other animals — you know, mating season or new babies or something — early summer things, anyway. I didn't think much about it, but just when I was going up to the tree, all of a sudden something hit me from behind. I heard Bess yelp, and then I must have blacked out. When I came to I didn't even think of Bess. I guess I might not even have remembered her."

He rubbed his dog's ears again and his voice choked a little. "I was very dazed. I guess I didn't notice that my sleeping bag and other things were gone, but I suppose they were, since you kids didn't find them. I do know that all I could think of was getting help, so I stumbled along one of the small paths to the road and then went along the road till I got to your place." He leaned down closer to Bess. "Sorry, girl," he murmured. "You must have been lying there hurt and I didn't even know it — didn't even know I'd had you with me."

His voice broke, and Louise put her hand on his arm.

"It's over now," she said gently, while Mom poured him more lemonade. "You and Bess are together again and you're both okay."

"Is there anyone you should notify?" Mom asked.

"Ohmigosh, my parents! Thank you! You're right. They live near me and they don't expect to hear from me very often when I'm hiking, but I still think I'd better call."

"There's a phone in the sitting room," said Mom. "I'll show you."

"So," said Nikki softly when he and Mom had left and Louise was clearing the glasses off the table, "whoever hit Michael on the head also kicked Bess and maybe hit her on the head, too. Otherwise she'd have followed him here, and..."

"Unless Bess was off having a drink of water or something when Michael came to," Travis interrupted. "Her head wasn't bashed in or anything."

"Right. But the important thing," Nikki went on, "is that whoever hurt Michael and Bess probably planted the fake scarab in his pack. And probably stole his sleeping bag and other stuff. We have our missing link, the thing that connects everything!"

"Yes, but we can't be sure about the bikes and the threats and stuff like that. And we still don't know who took the real scarab, do we? Or if they're even here."

"That's why we're setting a trap, in case they are."

"I'm so happy for that boy!" Louise came back from rinsing the glasses and sat down again just as Mom returned. Nikki could hear Michael's voice from the sitting room as he talked with his parents on the phone.

"We'd best tell the sheriff what he told us, though," Mom said.

"Or he should," Louise suggested. "I could drive him down to the office."

"Good idea. And that" — Mom looked sternly at Nikki and Travis — "is as far as we should go. I know we haven't found out who the real thief is. But we should let the sheriff handle it from now on."

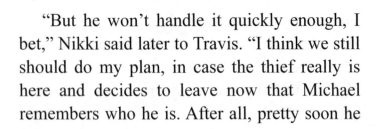

"But he won't handle it quickly enough, I bet," Nikki said later to Travis. "I think we still should do my plan, in case the thief really is here and decides to leave now that Michael remembers who he is. After all, pretty soon he might remember more about who hit him. And," she added, "we still can't be a hundred percent sure Michael isn't faking."

"Oh, come on," Travis said disgustedly. "Of course he isn't! Anyway, what's your plan?"

As Nikki told him, Travis began to grin, wider and wider.

CHAPTER 16
THE TRAP

"How splendid," Charley said when he and Don drove up to the inn as planned on their way back from picking up their new kitchen equipment. Nikki and Travis were outside walking Bess with Michael when they arrived. Michael told them his story, occasionally interrupted by Nikki and Travis. "That's absolutely wonderful!" Charley grabbed Michael's hand and shook it vigorously while Don stood by nodding, enthusiastically for him.

"So I'm afraid I won't be able to work in the kitchen after all," Michael said apologetically.

"I'm going to have to get back home pretty soon."

"That's perfectly all right," said Don, all business again. "We've managed this long. There's no reason why we can't go on managing."

But Charley was still bubbling. "Look," he said, "this calls for a celebration. I don't mean the fact that Michael won't be working for us, but the fact that he's figured out who he is. Of course you'll stay with us, though, Michael, till you do leave. And," he went on, after a quick look at Don, "we'd been thinking of asking Louise and Mindy if we could cater a meal up here at the inn, just to see if we could manage it. Business is slow in the winter until ski season, but we thought if we could go into the catering business, that might help tide us over. We could do a gala meal up here, if Mindy and Louise agree, and invite all the guests." He turned to Nikki and Travis. "What do you think?"

Travis looked skeptical but Michael said, "Sounds like fun."

Nikki, her mind working very fast, seized Charley's hand and said, "That's a great idea! It fits right in," she whispered to Travis.

"Huh?" he whispered back.

"With The Plan, stupid," she said impatiently. "It's a great idea," she said to Charley again. "We'll ask our moms, and we'll ask the guests, too."

"Engraved invitations would be nice," Charley said wistfully.

"Better slow down, Charley," Don said. "We can't afford that."

"We could make invitations," Nikki offered. "Travis is very good at printing. You should see the labels he puts on the drawings of his inventions."

"Splendid!" Charley spoke before Don could. "Good idea. But ask first," he added, taking Don's arm as they turned to go.

"Hang on a sec," Michael said. "Could we just make it a celebration in general, not all centered on me?"

"Maybe," Charley said doubtfully. "But it's not every day someone suddenly recovers from amnesia."

"I know," said Michael, "but it's embarrassing. Can't it just be in celebration of the first week of the inn? I'd really much rather."

"If you insist," Charley said. "Okay, Don?"

"Certainly," Don answered. "We wouldn't want to embarrass you."

"The inn hasn't been open a week yet," Nikki pointed out.

"We'll need a couple of days to prepare," Don said. "When's the week up?"

Nikki counted hastily on her fingers. "Monday."

Charley opened his arms as if embracing the world. "Perfect! We're not open Mondays anyway. You just call us as soon as you clear it with your moms, okay?"

"Okay," Nikki and Travis said together.

It was fine with the adult Taylor-Michaelsons.

Nikki worked out the details of her plan, and Travis got busy with the invitations. The elderly Woodwards, whom Nikki had hardly seen since they'd arrived, asked lots of questions but eventually accepted. Mrs. Tansy said she wasn't sure, because of little Abigail, but when Nikki said she could come, too, Mr. Tansy accepted for the three of them. And all the other guests, except Miss Dalrymple, who had to leave on Sunday, said they'd be delighted. "It's okay about Miss Dalrymple," Nikki confided to Travis, "since she's not a suspect anyway."

"Yeah," said Travis, "but what if we're wrong about that and she did do it? Maybe we've got the wrong suspects."

"I don't think so." But Nikki watched Miss Dalrymple carefully till Sunday just to make sure, and searched her room thoroughly as soon as she left. "She's clean," she told Travis afterwards. "I'm sure of it."

The big day finally arrived. Mom vacuumed the public areas — they still hadn't found a maid — and ironed the lace tablecloth and the linen napkins she'd gotten from her own mother years earlier. Travis dusted and polished the big dining room table, the sideboard, the chairs, and the silver candlesticks till they shone. Louise trimmed the bushes in front of the inn, weeded the front garden, and created a stunning flower arrangement, which Mom carefully put right in the center of the sideboard. And Nikki, after reluctantly washing the living room and dining room windows and the best china and glasses till they sparkled, set the trap — a neatly built display which she and Travis had finished on Sunday afternoon. It really was quite professional, like something in a craft show or even a museum — a simple pine stand, painstakingly varnished, with the fake scarab mounted in its center. A mirror fastened behind the scarab reflected it and caught the light.

Louise came into the dining room just as Travis was pushing the flowers to one end of the sideboard so Nikki could set up the display in the middle. "Think of it as a conversation piece," Nikki told her.

"It's bound to be that," Louise agreed, "but Mom isn't going to be happy about the flowers being moved."

"We could put the flowers on the table," Travis said.

Louise shook her head. "People won't be able to see each other then. Tell you what. You guys go and pick some more flowers — the same kinds — and make another arrangement just like this one to put at the other end of the sideboard. Then the whole thing will look symmetrical. Intentional, too, as if we planned it that way."

Nikki groaned. "I'm awful at arranging flowers."

"Me, too." Travis said.

"I'll help," Louise promised. "I don't know what you guys are up to, but I have an idea that whatever it is would be a lot more effective if it didn't look so obvious. It seems obvious now, because the flowers really look as if they belong in the center."

Travis eyed the sideboard. "Louise is right."

"Yeah," Nikki said. "I see what you mean. Okay. But please do help, Louise; we'll make a mess of it."

But they managed well enough and Mom agreed when Louise said, "That single vase looked unbalanced, Mindy, on one end with

Nikki and Travis's little — er — decoration in the middle."

Mom fingered the scarab lightly. "This does look pretty here, and the mirror's a clever idea. But why do I think there's more to this than I can see?"

"Because there probably is," said Louise.

Mom turned sternly to Nikki. "Is there?"

"Yes, sort of," Nikki admitted uncomfortably. "But it — it's safe."

"Perfectly safe," Travis said.

"And it does kind of honor Michael," Nikki added quickly. "I mean, he didn't want the dinner to celebrate his memory coming back, but there ought to be something to commemorate that, don't you think?"

"Oh, yes," Louise said solemnly. "Yes indeed." She sighed. "I think, Mindy," she said to Mom, "we'd better just wait and see what happens, don't you?"

"I guess. Assuming no one's going to let us in on the secret?"

"I think the fewer people who know, the better," Nikki said.

"I see. But I think," Mom continued, "that it

might be a good idea if we invited the sheriff tonight. Don't you, Louise?"

Louise nodded. "Good idea. I'll just go call him."

Mom stepped back and surveyed the display on the sideboard. "It certainly does look nice. Eye-catching." And with a somewhat forced-looking smile at Nikki and Travis, she followed Louise into the kitchen.

"It's okay," Nikki said to Travis. "It probably is a good idea to have the sheriff here. It could get rough, maybe. I don't know."

"I hope you're right. It sounds like a good plan, but I don't think the thief is going to say 'Oh, look, there's the fake scarab I put in Michael's pack to hide that I took the real one.' I wouldn't if I'd done it. What if he doesn't react at all?"

"Or she," Nikki corrected. "We're going to have to watch everyone very carefully. I'm hoping the thief will be surprised enough to give himself away. And ..."

"Or herself," Travis interrupted with an evil grin.

"Okay, okay," Nikki said impatiently. "And what I'm also hoping is that maybe that person will try to steal the scarab later, which means we might have to stay up all night."

"I don't mind that part. But why would the person want to steal the fake one if he already had the real one?"

"To plant it on someone else again. To throw the police off the trail of the real one. To save time. I don't know. Maybe it's not such a smart idea," she said, suddenly discouraged.

"It might work," Travis said kindly, patting Nikki's arm. "Besides, we've gone this far. We can't very well call it off now."

"No," said Nikki. "We can't."

Several hours later, Nikki, standing by the living room door rather stiffly in a green and yellow cotton dress, and Travis, also looking rather stiff in a tan summer suit with a red tie, greeted the guests as they came in.

Mr. Jordan, Suspect Number Four, was the first to come downstairs, in a plaid sport shirt and no jacket. "Good grief," he mumbled, staring at Travis through his thick glasses. "I didn't know this was to be that formal. I'll just go get a jacket..."

"No, no, please don't bother," said Louise, wearing a salmon-colored linen skirt and vest. "We want everyone to be comfortable. We get little enough chance to dress up," she went on, leading Mr. Jordan to the sofa, "and the children need to wear proper clothes at least once or twice a year. May I get you something to drink?"

Mr. and Mrs. Tansy were next, Mrs. Tansy with the baby in a basket. She looked rather flustered — pretty, too, in a softly flowing white dress sprigged with pale pink flowers. "At least little Abigail's not crying," she whispered to Nikki as she passed her. "Thank goodness. I do hope she won't spoil everything by fussing."

"She'll be fine, Irma," said her husband gruffly. "Just fine. Evening," he said to Mom, who came into the hall with a tray of glasses. "Nice night. Nice of you to have this party."

"Oh, no," said Mom. "It's nice of all of you to come."

The sheriff, in uniform, arrived as Mom ushered the Tansys into the living room. He winked at Nikki and Travis and lowered his voice as he said, "I hear you've got something planned. Your — er — folks thought I ought to be here. Maybe we can have a bit of a talk about it."

"Maybe," Nikki said politely.

There was a clattering from the kitchen, and soon after, Michael came nervously through the hall balancing a tray of fancy hors d'oeuvres. "Sorry for the noise," he said. "I decided to give Charley and Don a hand, but it's a good thing I'm not going to work for them. Turns out I'm clumsy around kitchens. I remember that, now, too, a bit late, though. Have some fish paste?" he said to Nikki. "No? These little bacon things are pretty good."

"Thanks." Nikki popped a bacon thing into her mouth. It wasn't bad. But Travis, who she saw had taken a fish paste one, was making an awful face. She tried not to giggle.

Elderly Mr. and Mrs. Woodward crept downstairs then and Nikki and Travis ushered them into the living room where they sat close together on the sofa, crowding Mr. Jordan a little. Mr. Woodward was wearing a blue shirt, which made Nikki punch Travis and nod toward it. "He can't be the one," Travis said under his breath. "He's too old. He can hardly walk!"

"Don't let appearances deceive you," Nikki said, trying to speak without moving her lips. "We'll have to keep an eye on him in the dining room."

The Woodwards were soon followed by the Cobbs, with Herbert Jr. in a brightly flowered shirt and a sleeveless sweater. "My mother made me wear this shirt," he whispered to Nikki and Travis as he passed them. "I hate it."

"You should," Travis whispered back.

Mr. Cobb had on a green shirt, Nikki noticed, not his blue one. Mr. Jordan wasn't wearing his blue shirt either. Only Mr. Woodward was in blue. And so far, none of the women wore blue either.

Miss Fletch, obviously just back from a rock-gathering expedition, stuck her head into the living room as they were discussing whether to start without her and Professor Zorich. "I'll be down in two shakes," she called cheerily from under her huge straw hat, waving her little hammer. "Just two shakes."

And by the time she did appear again — in the same blue skirt, Nikki noticed, that she'd worn when she'd arrived — Professor Zorich had arrived in a wrinkled brown suit and a white shirt that was clean but unironed. "No tie," Travis pointed out to Mom as they were all about to go into the dining room. He loosened his.

Nikki grabbed Travis's hand and pulled him into the dining room ahead of the guests, ignoring Louise's whispered admonition. "We've got to watch them as they come in," she said. "This is crucial. You stand there." She positioned Travis at one end of the sideboard, and she took up a post at the other.

"Oh," Miss Fletch cried as soon as she got to the door, with Professor Zorich close behind.

"Look! What a lovely decoration! Why," she said, going closer to the display on the sideboard, "that's really very like the scarab that was stolen." She gave Nikki and Travis a sharp look and then turned to Mom and Louise as Professor Zorich bent closer to the display, peering at it. "Wherever did you get it?"

"We — I — that is..." Mom began.

"We found it." Nikki stepped forward, her eyes darting around the room. Miss Fletch nodded, looking as if she'd like to say more, and while Michael told anyone who would listen about his amnesia, Nikki watched each entering guest as closely as she could, even though she realized Miss Fletch's outcry had removed the element of surprise on which she'd been counting. Mr. Jordan didn't look at the display at all — "which makes him," she whispered to Travis as soon as she could, "a suspect again." The Woodwards glanced at it and then embarked on a long story about a trip they'd taken to Egypt several years earlier. "When we could both get about more easily," Mrs. Woodward said at the end of it, patting her husband's arm.

The sheriff, as Nikki expected, barely acknowledged the scarab, but he winked.

Young Herbert Cobb poked at it, and said, "This is really cool. I'd like to sketch it, afterwards," but his father pulled him away and plunked him down next to his mother, who hadn't gone near the sideboard at all.

Professor Zorich finally turned away from the scarab and said, "Too bad there aren't any hieroglyphics on it, but I don't think they usually carved them on scarabs."

And then everyone gasped, for little Mrs. Tansy, last into the room with Mr. Tansy and Abigail as Professor Zorich turned away, swayed unsteadily by the door, nearly dropping the baby. As she fainted, her husband deftly caught both her and Abigail, and at the same time Mom and Louise leapt forward. "The doctor," Mom said. "I'll just call..."

"No, no," Mr. Tansy said hastily, and he whisked his wife and daughter out of the room; Nikki could hear him struggling up the stairs, talking to Mrs. Tansy in a low voice.

"Wow," Travis whispered as everyone stood

uncertainly around the table. "That's the second person who's fainted here!"

"Wow is right!" Nikki whispered back.

Mom was still over by the door, looking anxiously into the hall as if thinking about following the Tansys, but Louise cleared her throat and said, "Come along, folks. I'm sure Mr. Tansy knows what to do. We'll check in a few minutes if he doesn't come back. Meanwhile, do let's start." She gestured to the guests to sit down.

Slowly, one by one, the guests obeyed, but the festive mood had vanished, and Don served the soup in near silence. A few minutes later, Mr. Tansy returned. "Sorry," he said. "She's very embarrassed. She said she's afraid she's spoiled the party. But she'll be fine, just needs to rest. Please just go on eating." He peered into Miss Fletch's soup bowl, next to him. "Looks good! Is there any more?"

"Sure is." Don took the tureen over to him and ladled out a generous helping.

"Wouldn't Mrs. Tansy like something?" Mom asked. "We could give you some soup to take up to her."

"No, no," Mr. Tansy answered. "That's very kind. She's been very tired lately, since having the baby. She had a rough time, and the heat gets to her. I'd thought coming here might help build her up..." His voice broke, and Louise, patting his arm, offered him his water glass.

The meal was uneventful after that. It was also very good. Don, elegant in his maitre d' suit, came in bearing dish after splendid dish: a beautiful salad, with tomatoes and red and yellow peppers making bright splotches against assorted greens; two perfectly roasted ducks, crisp and brown; tiny potatoes, roasted with the duck; gravy and a sweet dark red sauce with berries in it. "For the duck," Don explained, carrying them in. "Do please try them both." Michael followed carefully in Don's wake, making several trips with bowls of vegetables and a platter of corn on the cob. He managed not to spill. "Though I was sure half the ears would roll off onto the floor," he confessed later to Nikki and Travis as they helped him clear away the main course.

Dessert, at which Mrs. Tansy appeared again, looking much better, was elegant puff pastries, filled with ice cream and topped with chocolate sauce and whipped cream. "It's just a sundae, really," Herbert Jr. remarked in a loud undertone to Nikki and Travis, "except for this thing underneath it. I'd like a brownie sundae better."

"Or just a plain one," said Nikki, agreeing with him for once. The pastry was flaky and dry, but the adults said they liked it.

Then there was coffee, or tea, or cocoa back in the living room. Charley, Don, and Michael joined the guests after bringing it in. No one seemed at all interested in the display any more, although several people commented again on the flowers. And all of them commented on the meal.

"So," Nikki whispered to Travis, "We're going to have to stay up all night after all."

CHAPTER 17
CAUGHT!

Much later that night, when the inn was quiet and everyone had gone to bed, Nikki and Travis, with Max, snuck warily downstairs, dark sweatshirts over their pajamas. They hid, one at each end of the sideboard, behind the long drapes that fell conveniently from the windows.

"What do we do if someone really does try to take the scarab?" Travis asked uncomfortably.

"I'm not sure," Nikki admitted.

"What if whoever it is finds us? What if they attack us?"

"That's why we've got Max." Nikki patted the dog. "He'll protect us, I'm pretty sure."

"Oh, right," Travis said scornfully. "Max wouldn't hurt anyone. Mom always says he'd lead a robber right to the TV and the silver."

"He'd protect us if someone were trying to hurt us." But Nikki sounded surer than she felt. "Shh, now. We've got to be very still and very quiet. Max, down. Stay."

With a sigh and a grunt, Max lay down beside Nikki at the far end of the sideboard.

Dim light came through the windows between the drapes, and shadows crept across the dining room table as the moon rose and sailed across the sky, glinting on polished wood and silver candlesticks, and making the scarab and its reflection in the mirror glow eerily blue. Nikki yawned and fought to stay awake. Her legs tingled from staying still, then almost cramped, and she could hear Travis's breathing getting slower and deeper from the other end of the sideboard. She was just about to whisper to him to wake up when a soft rustling sound caught her ear and she stiffened. So did Max.

"Psst," she said as quietly as she could. "Travis."

"I hear it," came Travis's voice, barely audible.

And suddenly the atmosphere in the dining room changed, as if the very air had become electric.

Softly, quietly, a dim white figure glided into the room, silent as a ghost. It looked like a ghost, in fact; it was wearing a long white garment. As Nikki strained to see who it was and at the same time put a restraining hand on Max, it floated over to the sideboard and slowly, very carefully, bent toward the faintly glowing scarab.

A hand — a long, slender hand — reached out to the scarab — lifted it from the display — cradled it ...

Nikki snapped on the light, and several things happened at once.

The person with the scarab screamed, dropping it to the floor. Nikki gasped and picked it up; Travis catapulted out of his hiding place, Max snarled, and from the hall came a louder growl and a man's gutteral cry.

"It's Mrs. Tansy!" Nikki cried in shocked disbelief, grabbing one of the woman's arms; Travis grabbed the other, and Max barked. Sounds of a tremendous struggle came from the hall. A moment later Mom and Louise dashed in from the kitchen end of the dining room; Michael, with Mr. Cobb firmly in his grip and Bess growling and baring her teeth beside him, burst in from the hall.

"I think I'd better call the sheriff," Louise said a little shakily, going past Michael, Mr. Cobb, and Bess into the hall.

"I'm sorry, I'm sorry!" moaned Mrs. Tansy as her husband dashed into the room, his face ugly with fury. "I ruined it. I thought if I just got this one, I could..."

"You fool!" her husband shouted. "You stupid fool! I told you to leave it!"

"It doesn't matter." Mr. Cobb sank wearily into the dining room chair to which Michael propelled him. "It doesn't matter any more." He groaned and put his hands over his face.

Mrs. Cobb, looking as if she was about to burst into tears, and Herbert Jr., looking almost as furious as Mr. Tansy, ran in then.

"Thanks," Herbert Jr. said bitterly to Nikki and Travis. "Oh, thank you very much. Why couldn't you mind your own business?" His voice broke and he turned, running straight into Professor Zorich, who'd just come into the room, rubbing his eyes sleepily. The professor caught Herbert Jr. and, obviously bewildered, held him against his chest. "There, there," he said absently, as Herbert sobbed. "What's all this about?" he asked Nikki and Travis severely as Louise came back in saying, "The sheriff's on his way."

"I'm not sure." Nikki felt a little shaky herself. She explained about the trap and then turned to Mrs. Tansy. "But I never suspected you!"

Mr. Cobb took his hands down from his face. "Don't blame her. She doesn't have the real scarab. It's not really her fault." He looked up at Michael, who was still gripping his shoulders firmly. "If you'll just let go of me for a minute..."

"Not on your life," Michael said, and Bess, the hair on the back of her neck still standing up, growled again, her eyes on Mr. Cobb. Max stood nearby, as if ready to help Bess if need be.

"Then at least reach into my left-hand pants pocket," said Mr. Cobb.

Michael did, and everyone gasped when he pulled out a turquoise scarab, exactly like the fake one Nikki was still holding.

Louise let out a low whistle and so did Michael. Mrs. Cobb gave a single sob and pulled Herbert Jr. close to her, away from Professor Zorich.

"My dad's not really a thief," said Herbert Jr. defensively, with a loud sniff. "Not any more."

"You'd better explain, Herbert." Mrs. Cobb went to her husband and put her hand on his shoulder next to Michael's hand; Michael edged his away a little, but he didn't let go.

Mr. Cobb sighed heavily. "Long ago," he said, "before I met my wife and settled down, I was a — I was an art thief. I had a good business, but then I was caught, and I did time in jail. When I got out, I'd learned my lesson, and soon afterwards I met Mary, here" — he reached up and squeezed his wife's hand —

"and married her. She likes art, too, so we always spent a lot of time in museums. I didn't have enough money any more to add to my — er — my private collection, but we enjoyed the few pieces I still had."

He paused and his wife handed him a handkerchief with which he wiped his glistening brow. "Thank you, dear," he said. "When we had Herbert Jr.," he went on, "and found out he was gifted, we sold the few pieces I had left so we could afford to send him to a special school for gifted kids. But this year they raised the tuition, and we'd just about run out of money. The only thing I could think of doing was going back to what I knew best. So I stole the scarab and had a fake one made in case I needed it to point suspicion at someone else or to throw people off the track of the real one. My wife and I had already agreed to meet the Tansys here in Bennet, but then when we arrived and heard that the sheriff was looking here for the scarab and the thief, I..."

"He was looking here," Nikki explained, interrupting, "because a museum guide found a map with the route to Bennet marked on it. The sheriff said it was right between the scarab's case and a couple of cat statues."

"So that's where I lost it!" Michael exclaimed. "It must've fallen out of my pack when I was taking a last look at those cats. I was studying their smooth lines — very fluid..."

"Well," said Mr. Cobb ruefully, "I wish you hadn't dropped it. I bet you do, too, because when I heard on the radio that the police had alerted the sheriff in Bennet, I realized I'd better plant my fake scarab on someone. And there you were, heaven sent, you might say, with your gear, in a convenience store we stopped at to look for a likely person. We'd come early, before our reservations, to look around for a good place to meet the Tansys privately; we didn't want to risk meeting in the inn. And like I said, there you were, so I followed you into the woods, and..."

"And," said Michael, "you planted the fake one on me, and bashed me over the head and kicked my dog..."

"Yes," said Mr. Cobb. "I'm sorry." He

looked sympathetically at Bess. "She's a good dog," he said sadly. "She was trying to defend you. She grabbed at my shirt, pulled it out..."

"The blue cloth," Nikki whispered to Travis, who nodded.

"...and ripped a piece of it right off."

"You could have killed her," Michael said angrily. "Or made me lose my memory for good."

"I didn't mean to hurt you. In fact, I didn't mean to hit you at all. I followed you and when you put down your gear to get some water from that little creek, I grabbed your small pack. I was about to put the fake scarab in it when you straightened up and I panicked." Mr. Cobb put his head in his hands. "I'm sorry."

"What about my sleeping bag?" Michael asked. "And the rest of my gear? And the mysterious questioner early in the morning in the hospital. Was that you?"

"And the threats on our car and on the phone," Nikki asked. "Were those you, too?"

"I can show you where your gear is," Mr. Cobb said to Michael. "Yes, it was me questioning you in the hospital early the next morning; I snuck in past the nurses. I was afraid you might die and when I saw that you weren't going to, I had to find out how much you remembered." He turned to Nikki. "Yes, the threats were from me. I was afraid you'd figure out what had happened. And," he said with a smile that was more wistful than bitter, "you darn near did."

"What about the bikes?" Travis asked. "Did you take them?"

Mr. Cobb nodded. "To slow you down. And to distract you if you found anything in the woods."

"The towels from Mr. Jordan's room?" Mom asked.

Mrs. Cobb cleared her throat. "Herbert's shoes were muddy," she said. "In fact, all his clothes were covered with mud. I was able to take his clothes to the laundromat in town, but I had to clean his shoes, and I didn't dare use the towels from our room." She bent down, hugging Herbert Jr., who was still sniffing. "I'm sorry about the towels. I didn't have time to take them to the laundromat, too. I'll replace them."

"Never mind," Louise said. "The towels are the least of it."

"That's why the funny clothes when you arrived," Nikki said suddenly to Mr. Cobb. "Because of the mud."

"Right," said Mr. Cobb.

"Were you really house hunting?" Louise asked.

Mrs. Cobb sniffed loudly. "Yes. But not seriously."

"We thought it would be a good way to justify our being here," said her husband.

"I don't understand," said Mom, "where Mrs. Tansy comes in. Why were you meeting the Tansys here?"

Mrs. Tansy gave a sniff, and suddenly seemed a lot stronger than the weak, rather fluttery woman she'd seemed before. "I'm a fence," she said bluntly. "I was going to sell the real scarab for the Cobbs, giving them most of the money and keeping a percentage for myself."

"You're a fence?" Louise asked incredulously.

"Yes," she said, rather proudly, Nikki thought. "Herbert and I are old friends. When I saw the little display the children made, I thought maybe there still was a way to get the fake scarab back. I wanted to help Herbert out. Do him one last favor, you might say."

Mr. Tansy turned away, shaking his head and muttering.

"How come you wanted the fake scarab?" Nikki asked.

"So I could put it where the sheriff would find it," Mrs. Tansy said. "I hoped that might give us enough time to get away and sell the real one. I wasn't sure how much all of you knew about it, though."

"Did you really faint?" asked Travis.

"No, of course not," said Mrs. Tansy. "That was to throw everyone off and to give me time to plan. So was my being — weak, before."

There was a sudden pounding at the front door and a moment later the sheriff and two other men charged into the room. "Hold it right there," the sheriff thundered like someone on TV. "No one move!"

Everyone slept late the next morning. And by the time Nikki and Travis got up, Miss Fletch, Mr. Jordan, and the Woodwards had left. When Nikki came sleepily down the stairs she found Professor Zorich in the kitchen sipping coffee with Mom, Louise, Michael, and a very shaky-looking Herbert Jr. Snowball, as usual, watched from the refrigerator, and Max and Bess snoozed companionably under the table.

"Good morning," Louise said, handing Nikki a glass of orange juice. "Travis still asleep?"

Nikki stepped aside; Travis was right behind her.

"Where are Mr. and Mrs. Cobb?" Travis asked, accepting a glass of juice himself.

"The sheriff sent them to Boston late last night," Michael explained. "After he took them away from here. And the real scarab is on its way back to the museum."

Mom laid a hand gently on Herbert Jr.'s arm. "The Cobbs will have to stand trial."

"That's tough, Herb," Travis said. He sounded almost sincere.

Herbert Jr. sniffed loudly. His eyes were red as if he'd been crying.

"What about Herbert's school?" asked Nikki.

Mom smiled. "The professor has offered to pay for it. And to drive Herbert to an aunt's, where he'll be able to stay till everything's been resolved."

"We'll be back here next vacation, Herbert and I," said the professor, standing up and putting a hand on Herbert Jr.'s shoulder. "To see if we can figure out what it says on that ogham stone of yours. Herbert's got a fine mind. It would be a pity not to go on educating it. The boy could go far. Not," he added, looking severely at him, "in his parents' footsteps, however."

"I don't think they'll ever do anything bad again," Herbert Jr. said in a very small voice as Professor Zorich steered him to the door.

"Neither," said Louise, "do I." She got up and gave Herbert Jr. a hug. "Good luck, Herbert."

"Hang in there, Herb," Michael said as Herbert Jr. and the professor left.

"Yes," Mom called after them, "good luck, dear. We'll look forward to having you and the professor stay with us again."

Nikki looked at Travis, who rolled his eyes.

"What's this?" asked Travis when they were gone. He pointed to two shiny objects lying on the table.

"The sheriff left them for you," said Michael. "Honorary deputy badges. And he said you may keep the fake scarab."

Louise picked up the badges, handing one to Travis and one to Nikki. "He said that without you two, they might never have caught the Cobbs."

"And," said Mom, "when you've had your breakfasts, the local newspaper wants you to give them a call. They want to interview you."

"You're famous," said Michael.

"And you've been here only a week," Louise added. "What amazing kids we have, Mindy!"

Mom gave them each a hug. "You can say that again," she said.

Vigorously, Max wagged his tail.